'Exactly ho...
Maggie?'

Slane's mouth l...
hers, crushing h...
not the slightest ...

It was like coming home, she thought incredulously as she lifted her arms and clung to him,
her body rejoicing in the swift surge of desire
it encountered in his with an abandon that
brought a soft groan bursting from him. When
he began drawing her from him, her impassioned resistance brought another groan—
almost of pain—as he forced her away and
held her at arm's length.

'No,' he protested hoarsely. 'This won't work!
We hardly know any more about one another
than we did last time.'

Kate Proctor is part Irish and part Welsh, though she spent most of her childhood in England and several years of her adult life in Central Africa. Now divorced, she lives just outside London with her two cats, Florence and Minnie, presented to her by her two daughters who live fairly close by. Having given up her career as a teacher on her return to England, Kate now devotes most of her time to writing. Her hobbies include crossword puzzles, bridge and, at the moment, learning Spanish.

Recent titles by the same author:

TALL, DARK AND DANGEROUS

A PAST
TO DENY

BY
KATE PROCTOR

MILLS & BOON

MILLS & BOON and the Rose Device
are trademarks of the publisher.
Harlequin Mills & Boon Limited,
Eton House, 18–24 Paradise Road, Richmond, Surrey TW9 1SR

© Kate Proctor 1996

ISBN 0 263 79481 4

Set in 10 on 12 pt Linotron Times
01-9605-54755

Typeset in Great Britain by CentraCet, Cambridge
Made and printed in Great Britain

CHAPTER ONE

MAGGIE WALLACE sat cross-legged on the bed, haphazardly drying her hair. Cocooned in the luxury of Professor Connor Fitzpatrick's elegant Dublin home, she gazed through the rain-splattered window into the stormy darkness beyond with cosy contentment.

It was a shame that her stay had to coincide with the Prof's trip to America, she reflected lazily, before giving a wry grin and deciding that it was probably just as well, given their shared penchant for staying up half the night, chatting.

The smile abruptly left her attractive features as she remembered the state in which she had been when the Prof had rung her, announcing a problem that had cropped up which he'd hoped she would help him solve.

Once again, albeit unknowingly, the Prof had come to her rescue, she mused despondently, then gave an angry shake of her head. No, she didn't *need* rescuing any more, she told herself firmly, leaning forward and sweeping her shoulder-length dark blonde hair up over her face. She switched the hair-dryer up a notch and dried off the damp underneath parts, but the unsettling thoughts lingered on.

All right, so it had taken far too long, she argued defensively, but she had already begun looking to the future before Peter had turned up out of the blue and momentarily knocked her tentative reawakening sideways. And the fact was that it had actually proved to be a blessing in disguise in that now she could feel the future beckoning her with added strength.

Maggie switched off the hair-dryer and groaned at the distant sound of the telephone ringing. In a house this size any normal person would have at least a couple of extensions, she grumbled to herself as she flew down the stairs to the study, but not the Prof— with his negative attitude to telephones, it was a wonder he actually had one at all.

'Connor, I hope your ears are burning!' she exclaimed when she heard the soft tones of the distinguished Irish academic greet her. 'I nearly broke my neck getting down the stairs to answer this.'

'The exercise will do you good, darling,' he chuckled. 'So tell me, has the lad arrived?'

'Lad?' queried Maggie. 'If you mean the Fitzpatrick Consolidated chemist, he hasn't contacted me yet.'

'No—Slane. I could wring that young devil's neck,' complained Connor. 'The one time I'm in his part of the world he takes off for Dublin.'

'Slane? I take it we're talking the Yankee Fitzpatrick Slane?' Maggie drew the receiver back from her ear as a roar of laughter assaulted it from across the Atlantic.

'The very one,' chortled the professor. 'My late cousin James's boy, and not simply one of that filthy capitalist lot from the other side of the Atlantic I keep telling you about, but the *numero uno* Yankee Fitzpatrick.'

'It would serve you right if they cut you off without a penny, the way you talk about them,' laughed Maggie. Back when they had first met, and for no reason that she could really explain, she had been surprised to discover just how closely related the professor was to the powerful American family that owned Fitzpatrick

Consolidated—one of the wealthiest and most commercially ruthless of the big American corporations.

'Stop sidetracking me, girl,' grumbled the professor, his aversion to the telephone beginning to assert itself. 'The point is there's been a change of plan—it's Cousin Slane you'll be assistant to for the tests and—'

'Connor, I hope you're joking!' exclaimed Maggie, her alarm sensors shrieking into overdrive. 'You told me this would be an opportunity for me to take a couple of weeks to brush up on my rusty lab technique, not that I'd be involved in something so important that the big boss of Fitzpatrick Con—'

'Maggie, you'll be dissecting a few plants, damn it,' cut in Connor. Then he added with a sigh, 'I suppose, now that I think on it, I'm not at all surprised young Slane's decided to get involved... And there's also the fact that it gives him an excuse to return to Ireland, which—'

'Why would he need an excuse?'

'He hasn't been to Dublin since Marjorie's funeral,' he said, his voice catching at the mention of his beloved wife, 'and, believe me, he worshipped her... Damn it, this will be a doubly hellish trip for him—and here I am stuck on the Yankee side of the Atlantic.'

'Hellish?' exclaimed Maggie, wondering what on earth she was about to be let in for.

'Pay no heed to me, darling,' he responded, discomfiture ringing in his tone. 'You might not remember, but James died just six months before Marjorie. Anyway, forget these old man's ramblings of mine and just rest assured that Slane possesses one of the finest scientific minds there is.

'Come to think of it, I should be giving thanks he'll be putting it to its rightful use for a while, even if it is on something this elementary, instead of squandering it on running that damned company.'

'Are you sure he hasn't deliberately picked a time to return when you'll not be here?' teased Maggie, only too willing to follow his lead in lightening the subject. 'Excuse me a moment—I thought I heard something.'

It was the sound of a car drawing away, followed by muffled movement in the area of the porticoed porch. 'I've a feeling your illustrious cousin has just arrived. I'd better let him in.'

'Connor, you old devil, where are you?' bellowed an American-accented voice from the hallway.

'Too late—he's already in, and bellowing for you.'

'Damn it, I'll never get off this wretched contraption,' grumbled Connor. 'I'd better have a word with him.'

'Mr Fitzpatrick,' called Maggie, putting down the receiver and running over to the study door. 'The professor's on the phone and would like a word with you.'

It all happened in a blur—the tall, dark-coated figure striding past her to pick up the receiver she had placed on the desktop and the sensation of her world crashing to pieces around her.

It was a trick of the light, a voice inside her shrieked from amidst the chaos breaking out within her—the room was in virtual darkness save for the small desk lamp angled uselessly across the blotter... Then he spoke, not in the raised tones that had issued from the hall and struck no chord in her, but in softly exasperated tones that were her complete undoing.

'That's great, Connor—me here and you there... No, I haven't seen Mom; I just got back in from

Australia a couple of days ago and... OK, OK...
Right, I *am* listening.'

His dark-lashed blue eyes rose as he listened and
alighted on Maggie, standing immobile a few steps
from the doorway.

'Damn it, Connor, you must have a pretty good idea
why I'm here!' he exploded suddenly, and turned
slightly, lowering his voice. 'And I'm not about to act
as surrogate instructor to some student you've taken
under your wing.'

Although Maggie was no longer able to see his face,
her mind's eye took over and she was able to conjure
up every last detail: the blue-blackness of his hair,
tousled almost to curliness; eyebrows arching in elegant
symmetry above heavy-lidded, lushly lashed eyes; the
nose, fine-boned and patrician, in perfect proportion to
the rest of those faultless features; the mouth, wide and
dramatically defined in its intriguing blend of harshness
and sensuality... The face of the stranger whose body,
one night long ago, had time after impossible time
possessed her own in a mindless frenzy of rapture.

'OK, Connor, you have me convinced,' he said, his
tone softening with affection. 'No problem—it's just
that right now I'm jet-lagged and dead on my feet...
Yeah, all I need is some of Mrs Morrison's food in me
to restore me—that and a bed to fall into.'

Maggie felt herself sway. Bed...cool linen sheets
slipping from glistening, passion-driven bodies to lie
rumpled on the floor.

'Perhaps you should tell her that for yourself.' The
laugher-filled words cut across the madness of Maggie's
wandering thoughts. 'OK, OK, I'll do that... And you
have yourself a good time—and give Mom my love

when you see her... No, she doesn't know anything about this; I'll tell her when I get back.'

He put the phone down, then dragged his hands wearily across his face before turning his attention to Maggie, who still stood where he had passed her, her body rooted to the spot by a petrifying mixture of horror and incredulity.

'Hi, Maggie—I'm Slane. I guess that's about the only place for us to start,' he muttered, tiredness hoarsening his voice.

No, thought Maggie dazedly, the deal had been no names...complete anonymity. She wanted to protest, but remained frozen as everything slurred into slow motion and he began walking towards her, his hand outstretched.

She was too busy steeling herself for the impact of his belated recognition to have any consciousness of how her hand came to be briefly enfolded in the cool clasp of his. It was beyond her comprehension that she might have given it freely.

'Look, whatever you heard me say to Connor,' he said, the familiarity of his voice washing over her like an intimate caress, seeking out and threatening to expose those secrets whose very existence made her feel that she could more easily die than acknowledge them, 'ignore it—apart from the fact that I'm dog-tired and jet-lagged.'

A state, in fact, in which his memory would be functioning well below par, reasoned Maggie—the idea that he actually might not have recognised her suddenly proving almost as impossible to accept as that of seeing him again—especially with regard to a woman he had met only once almost three years ago.

'I can see we need to talk,' he murmured, his eyes

for a split second catching hers, their look momentarily confounding her with the certainty that he had recognised her. 'I've plainly upset you.'

'And what makes you think that?' The coolness of that utterance astounded her; there was no way she could accept that it had emerged from her own traumatised person.

'Come on now, Maggie—even aside from the fact that it's written all over you, you hadn't been able to bring yourself to utter a word to me until just now.'

'I'd have looked a bit of an idiot trying to strike up a conversation wtih you, given that you've been on the phone to Connor ever since you walked in here.' She was about to disintegrate into a gibbering wreck, she thought dazedly, yet once again she had managed to sound the epitome of cool composure. 'But you're right about one thing—we need to talk.'

'Have you any objection to our doing that over coffee?' he asked, tiredness once more hoarsening his tone.

'No, of course not!' she exclaimed, her momentary certainty evaporating. 'I'll make some. . .and I suppose we should do something about finding a room for you, though I'm afraid I haven't a clue where the Prof keeps bedlinen and things.'

'Don't worry, I do,' he murmured, his mouth quirking with humour. 'And I still have my own room here, even though it's a good while since I've used it.'

Maggie's legs were shaking beneath her as she led the way to the kitchen and her mind had also started playing horrifying tricks on her which she was ruthlessly suppressing.

'My God, nothing's changed,' he muttered to himself, pausing to gaze around the large, comfortable kitchen

before slumping down on one of the chairs, still hud-
dled in his coat.

'How do you like your coffee?' asked Maggie, still
thrown by how remarkably well her mind was working,
seemingly independently of herself.

'Exactly twice as strong as Connor drinks his,' he
replied, with a chuckle that slid over Maggie like warm
silk and made her lose control of the thoughts she had
been so frantically suppressing. 'But you don't have to
wait on me,' he added, rising. 'I can make it myself.'

'You stay where you are—you look exhausted,' said
Maggie. 'I'll hang up your coat if you like; you must be
sweltering in it.'

It horrified her that she should even have mentioned
his taking anything off, given the images she was
battling to banish from her mind—of a body, golden
and stark naked and as awesomely perfect as that of a
Greek god—the body of this man as she had once seen
it and now kept seeing it. . .because her deranged mind
kept stripping it of the clothing adorning it.

'I'll keep it on a while,' he muttered. 'I guess my
body's as out of sync as my head is—I feel a bit cold.'

'Perhaps you should have a bath,' she said, sympathy
creeping into her voice as she handed him a large mug
of coffee. 'Would you like milk and sugar?'

'No, this is fine, thank you.'

Maggie poured her own coffee and went to the fridge
for milk, her movements slow as she played for time to
search for reason amongst the chaos of her thoughts.
The sympathy in her tone had irritated her, but really
there were no grounds for her to feel antagonism
towards him. . .apart, perhaps, from those of wounded
pride. After a night such as they had shared, how could
he possibly not remember?

She took her mug and sat down opposite him. 'We might as well get straight to the point,' she said. 'It's obvious I'm not the right person for the work that—'

'Connor says you are,' he cut in coolly. 'And you must have agreed, otherwise why are you here?'

'I'm here because the research student Connor had originally lined up had to drop out at the very last moment. Look, I don't know what Connor said to you, but the truth is I haven't been anywhere near a lab since I left university, so I'm hardly the person to be assisting someone in your position.'

'My position? Hell, all we're talking about here is dissecting a few plants, not who or what I am. And how come you felt able to assist a guy employed by the company I run, but not me?'

'Forgive me for sounding naïve,' snapped Maggie, 'but, if that's all it is, how is it that the managing director—or whatever it is you are—of a concern as vast as Fitzpatrick Consolidated is dealing with it personally?'

'Don't tell me you've never given in to a whim, Maggie.'

Instead of rounding on him in fury as her every instinct demanded, Maggie raised her mug to her lips. His words had been loaded to the hilt. . . Yet, on the other hand, his expression had been utterly blank. She took several sips of her coffee as confusion seeped its way into every pore of her being.

'Well, *I* didn't happen to come here on a whim,' she eventually responded stiffly. 'I came here because the Prof persuaded me I'd be helping him out of a fix, and that I'd also benefit from the experience.'

'And you're happy to help Connor out of a fix but not me—is that what you're saying?'

'No, of course not! I. . .look, I—I don't care wh-what either you or Connor say,' stammered Maggie, 'the mere fact that someone like you would involve himself in the donkey work tells me that this project is a million miles away from anything run-of-the-mill.'

He dragged his hands wearily across his face. 'I guess a bus ride could be described as pretty run-of-the-mill,' he sighed. 'There again, the reason for it being taken could make it anything but.'

Maggie heard his words, but it was the faint hint of Irish brogue that had momentarily slipped into them which caught her attention, striking a chord in her that sent her thoughts careering off at a tangent. She hadn't noticed it at first, all those years ago, and even when she had later it hadn't consciously struck her as being Irish—that soft lilt interwoven into his husky words of passion. . .

She gave an almost angry toss of her head. 'Well, whatever your reasons for being here, I'm sure someone like you won't have too much difficulty finding a suitably qualified lab assistant,' she stated firmly, rising.

'I'd have insurmountable difficulty,' Slane told her quietly. 'I don't have the contacts Connor has here, and even his are pretty sparse, with him having been in England so long. Besides, you were his second choice. If you pull out the project will have to be scrapped until next year.'

'That's ridiculous,' protested Maggie, suddenly feeling horribly trapped.

'There's nothing ridiculous about it,' he replied, with a barely perceptible shrug. 'The only complicated thing about these tests is the time factor involved—and that happens to be crucial. . . What exactly did Connor tell you about the project?'

Maggie sat back down on her chair, her head swimming. 'Nothing much,' she replied, 'except that the plant involved was on the verge of extinction and a botanist here had managed to reproduce it. He also mentioned that this plant was alleged to contain some miraculous property or other, though he seemed somewhat sceptical about that and didn't enlarge on what it was.'

'His scepticism is in no way misplaced,' muttered Slane, once again dragging his hands wearily across his face. 'But, if a minor miracle could be the end result, I guess it has to be worth a try.'

His own undisguised scepticism brought a startled look from Maggie, which in turn elicited a wry smile from her companion—a smile which, innocuous thought it was, sent a surge of unequivocally sexual longing blasting through her.

'Or don't you agree?' he persisted, his smile, as it softened into a coaxing one, wreaking further havoc within her.

'I. . . O-of course I agree,' she stammered, hot colour rushing to her cheeks.

'But?'

'But nothing,' she muttered, part of what Connor had said earlier ringing in her head. 'I'll stay.'

'What—you'll stay and assist me?' he asked, his eyes wary.

'Well, I certainly didn't mean I was going to keep house for you,' she snapped, appalled that she hadn't stopped to think twice before committing herself.

To her complete surprise he slumped forward, burying his face in his arms, convulsed with laughter.

'You might not find it quite so amusing when I tell

you that as from today Mrs Morrison is off on a two-week visit to her sister in Galway.'

He groaned as he raised his head. 'You may not believe this, but I have spent a number of years fantasising about sampling Mrs Morrison's cooking again,' he protested. 'Hell, I'm almost tempted to pack my bags and go back home,' he added, with a grin.

'Except that you haven't unpacked them yet,' pointed out Maggie, finding it impossible to keep her face straight, and even more impossible to do anything about the mind-blowing effect he had on her every time he smiled.

'You can't wait to be rid of me, can you, Maggie?' His words were teasing, but there was a deeper element of mockery in his eyes... Or was that simply her imagination?

'I've a nasty feeling you're going to be the one who can't wait to get rid of me once you're faced with exactly how rusty my lab skills are,' she stated woodenly. 'But as for Mrs Morrison's cooking—there's one of her magnificent concoctions in the oven, just waiting to be heated.'

Laughter burst unchecked from her as he clutched at his heart and rolled his eyes theatrically. There had been so many things about him that had attracted her even before the physical element had engulfed her, she thought with dismay—so why should anything be different now?

She rose to her feet. 'Why don't you get your things sorted and have a shower?' she suggested, her own aplomb still a source of amazement to her. 'And I'll get the food under way.'

He rose from the table. 'Maggie, I... Thanks,' he

muttered disjointedly. He hesitated as though about to say more, then turned and walked from the room.

For several seconds Maggie stood there, immobile in body and mind. When her body at last reactivated itself she switched on the oven, then prepared potatoes and carrots. By the time the potatoes were boiling she had cut the carrots into thin strips. . .and still her mind had not responded. Great, she told herself numbly, my mind's packed up on me.

Close to tears, she marched over to the cooker, threw a lump of butter, some sugar and a cupful of chicken stock she'd found in the fridge into a shallow pan and added the carrots. Then she gave a dazed shake of her head. What on earth had possessed her to attempt her mother's glazed carrots, she asked herself incredulously, when she only had the vaguest idea how to do them?

She slammed the lid onto the pan then walked to the back door, opened it and stepped out into the freezing night air.

A couple of months ago, when autumn had already begun yellowing the leaves on the trees that it would soon strip bare, something had begun stirring in her, she reflected, the thought still peculiarly tinged with detachment. It wasn't simply that circumstances had forced her into taking decisions regarding her life. . .it was more that the need burgeoning in her had happened to coincide with a change of circumstance in her working life; the effect—or, rather, the ultimate lack of effect—that Peter's reappearance had had on her was proof enough of that.

But for almost the past three years she might just as well have been asleep for all the living she had done, she concluded bitterly, then took a step back towards

the doorway as the wind suddenly changed direction
and sent rain whipping against her. She drew a hand
down her face, uncertain whether the wetness it
encountered was from the rain, her own tears or a
mixture of both.

And now what? she asked herself bleakly. She had
tried to deny the past out of existence for almost three
years, and it hadn't worked. OK, so she had to face it,
but *how* was the question, when the man who com-
prised such a large part of it had either forgotten her
or was deliberately not facing it himself... And the
answer wasn't exactly leaping out at her.

'Hey—Maggie!'

She jumped, startled not just by his voice but also by
his tone of open censure. She stepped inside and was
about to pull the door closed behind her when the acrid
smell of burning hit her.

'Don't, for God's sake, close that door,' ordered
Slane irritably as he strode across the kitchen and slung
the pan containing the carrots into the sink. 'And it
might have been an idea to turn the darned things off
before you started trying to clear the air,' he muttered,
leaning forward and throwing open the window above
the sink.

'I'm sorry, I thought I had turned them off,' lied
Maggie, automatically avoiding the truth and all its
accompanying complications... As usual, she noted
bitterly as she watched him stride back to the cooker,
his tall figure, now clad in jeans and a large sweatshirt,
oozing casual elegance. 'It's all right, I'll see to the
potatoes,' she said as he lifted the lid from the pan.

'There isn't much in the way of potato left for you to
see to,' he informed her baldly, stepping out of her way
as she approached.

Her cheeks burning with mortification, Maggie took the pan to the sink and resignedly watched most of the potatoes disappear down it when she drained them. She returned to the cooker, her eyes studiously avoiding the tall figure now engrossed in laying the table, turned up the heat in an attempt to dry out the mush in the pan, added a lump of butter to it and attacked the lot with the potato masher.

The silence ringing in her ears like pealing bells, she transferred the potatoes to a heated bowl, relieved to find that they were now of a consistency that required a spoon, instead of simply being poured.

By the time she had everything on the table she was feeling light-headed, wobbly-legged and not in the least like facing food, despite the tempting aroma emanating from the casserole. . .and even less like sharing a meal with the man seated opposite her, who had amusement plastered all over his face as he leaned over and began serving.

'Did you know Marjorie?' he startled her by asking.

She shook her head, the Prof's words about this being a double ordeal for him filling her mind just as they had in the moments before she had recklessly said she would stay. 'I wish I had. Connor's told me so much about her—she sounds a very special person.'

'Oh, Marjorie was special all right,' he said, his eyes momentarily clouding. 'In a funny way you reminded me of her just now.' He glanced up at her with an apologetic grin. 'Though, to be fair to you, had it been Marjorie in charge of these carrots the house would have been burned to a cinder.'

Maggie felt herself relax slightly; she even managed a smile. 'I do seem to remember Connor mentioning something about Mrs Morrison trying to ban her from the kitchen soon after they were married. But, I promise you, that was a first for me.'

'So how did you meet Connor?' he asked. 'I notice you sometimes refer to him as "the Prof", but I'd have thought you were too young to be one of his students.'

'Actually, I was one of his students in my final year in London,' she replied, her minding skidding away from other thoughts about that particular year. 'I was lucky; I was a member of one of his last groups before he retired fully.'

'Well, now I *am* impressed,' murmured Slane, his eyes widening in mock awe. 'So you made it into one of those *crème de la crème* groups he now and then indulged himself in before finally sliding into what he inaccurately refers to as "full retirement".'

'I know exactly what you mean,' said Maggie. 'He'll never really retire—that's the way he is.'

'Are you trying to change the subject?' asked Slane, a lazy grin softening any trace of harshness from his features. 'You know, your being one of Connor's chosen few really does set you apart from the mob. I guess any errors made in these tests we're about to do won't be down to you.'

'I wouldn't bet on that,' she muttered, and gave her full attention to her food, appalled by the burning, meltingly erotic sensation now churning inside her.

Shock could do terrible things, she told herself edgily, not certain that the monumental one to which she had been subjected hadn't destroyed her mental capacities altogether.

'I guess I should be filling you in about the tests— not that there's much to tell,' he said after a while. 'But I'm not sure I could get my head round it right now.' He glanced over at Maggie as he spoke, and for one brief moment she was certain that she saw a flash of mocking recognition in those heavy-lidded eyes; then they drooped in unmistakable exhaustion and her certainty yet again evaporated.

'That's understandable,' she said, rising to clear the dishes. 'You've had a lot to contend with today; we'll leave it until tomorrow.' Even before the words were fully out she sensed that they were a mistake. 'There's fruit if you'd like some,' she added hastily as the ambiguity of her words belatedly hit her. 'I'll make some coffee.'

'Just the coffee will be fine,' he said, his handsome face drawn with exhaustion as he leaned back in his chair, his eyes barely focusing as they followed her movements. 'So, I've had a lot to contend with today, have I?' he enquired.

It was the steely note in his tone that made Maggie freeze with apprehension.

'It was just that Connor mentioned you hadn't been back here since his wife died,' she stated woodenly.

'And that's all?' The note of challenge was undisguised.

Maggie switched on the kettle, playing for time as she fought to control the anger suddenly blazing within her. Perhaps he *was* only asking if that was all Connor had mentioned...perhaps not. Mortifying in the extreme though the idea was that he might have mentally erased the passion they had once shared, the idea that he was simply playing cat-and-mouse with her made her blood boil.

Unable to contain herself, she spun round to confront him. His head was tilted back and his eyes were closed. It wasn't the expression of weariness on his face that shrivelled the anger in her, but the anguish with which it was interlaced.

'He said that you loved her very much,' she stated quietly, turning away from his pain to attend to the coffee. And Connor had also mentioned his father's death, she reflected unhappily, feeling the ghosts of what had once been a scarcely bearable anguish stir within her.

It had been six long years since her own beloved father had died, and despite the healing process of time there were still moments when she could be taken unawares and become engulfed by a suffocating sense of loss. The expression she had witnessed on Slane Fitzpatrick's face was one with which she could not help but empathise.

'Yes, I loved Marjorie,' he said, straightening as she brought the coffee to the table. 'It would have been difficult not to,' he added, his eyes clouding over.

She had no idea what connection his coming to Ireland could have with his father, but Maggie felt certain that it wasn't Marjorie alone occupying his bleak thoughts. Because she could think of nothing she could trust herself to say, she picked up her cup and slowly drank from it. When it was empty she rose to her feet.

'I've a couple of letters I have to write,' she said, walking over to the dishwasher and starting to stack it, 'so I'll just get this cleared—'

'Leave those; I'll see to them—you've waited on me enough as it is.'

'Of course I haven't been waiting on you,' protested Maggie, closing the dishwasher and turning. 'You look all in—in fact, you don't look as though you'll last much longer.'

His eyes met hers, another of those lazy, disturbingly disruptive grins sauntering across his lips. 'You get off to your letters, Maggie, and don't be deceived by appearances,' he murmured. 'This guy has reserves of stamina you'd never believe.'

His words poleaxed her and it was left to that other, miraculously detached Maggie to take over, mouthing a polite goodnight and urging her leaden limbs from the room.

It was only when she had closed her bedroom door behind her that her real self re-emerged and her violently trembling body sagged against the wall. There was no way that his remark could have been an innocent coincidence... It couldn't simply be her imagination that he had just reminded her of the stamina which had enabled him to make love to her time after time that night long ago...or could it?

'This is impossible,' he had groaned at one stage during that passion-filled night, when insatiable hunger had flamed between them yet again. 'What have you done to me?'

And, even though she had been sexually innocent until that same night, she had instinctively known that what was happening between her and the beautiful stranger was an impossibility.

She gave a dazed shake of her head as she straightened her still violently trembling body and then stumbled towards the bed.

That night she had needed the magic of something impossible to heal her vicious wounds...but the cure had come close to destroying her.

CHAPTER TWO

WHEN she first awoke Maggie lay immobile, willing herself back to sleep, convinced that it was still the middle of the night. When her body failed to respond she checked the time and gave a disbelieving groan. As far as she was concerned, five-thirty in the morning *was* practically the middle of the night.

She hadn't even had to contend with the horrors of the day before seeping slowly back into her waking mind; she had woken with those horrors fully intact. And oddly enough it had been memories of her father that had filled her thoughts during the long hours in which sleep had eluded her. But other memories began stirring within her now—ones so long buried away and ruthlessly ignored that now there could be no holding them back.

His ice maiden. . . That was what Peter had so often called her—with what she had mistakenly read as teasing affection—and her lack of any real feelings of physical desire for him had always troubled her during those months when she had believed herself to be in love with him.

Yet, even without such feelings ever having been aroused in her, she had instinctively known that within her lay a capacity for passion that would one day overwhelm her. Crazy though it seemed to her now, she had actually managed to convince herself that, given time, it would be Peter who would eventually find the key to unlock those untapped passions. . .

But it had been, quite literally, a tall, dark stranger who had produced that elusive key, effortlessly unleashing in her what the man she had once believed she loved had imagined could be forced from her.

And now her knight, in his tarnished armour, lay sleeping just a few doors away from her, she reminded herself bitterly, and with apparently no recollection of their shared night, let alone any understanding of the powers his body still held over hers.

With a stifled cry of protest she sat up, shaking her head violently. She didn't want to be a freak! What she wanted was to be able to experience in the arms of a man she loved the same rapture she had known in those of Slane Fitzpatrick. Yet, in the almost three years that had passed, she hadn't found a man she could love, and those forbidden fires had remained dormant within her. . .until Slane's lazy grin had put a torch to them.

She leapt from the bed, threw on her dressing gown and stumbled down the stairs. It was just as she was entering the kitchen that the aroma of freshly brewed coffee wafted to her.

'Would you care for some coffee?' asked Slane, glancing up from what he was doing. Clad in a dark velour robe, a shadowy blue-blackness on his unshaven face, he looked drawn and tired and unspeakably attractive. 'I've just fixed it,' he added, getting out more crockery before Maggie had a chance to respond.

'Thanks,' she muttered, sagging down onto a chair. It hadn't occurred to her that he might be up, she thought fuzzily, then decided that that was no wonder, considering what an ungodly hour it was. 'I'm surprised you're up,' she added. 'I thought you'd be catching up on sleep.'

'So did I,' he murmured wryly, passing her a large cup of black coffee, 'but my body refused to play ball.' He sat down opposite her, his eyes flickering with amusement over her somewhat dishevelled figure. 'It's good to have company, though. I guess you must be one of those people Connor refers to as "larks"—up with the birdies and bright as a button.'

'Ha, ha,' muttered Maggie, then took a swig of coffee and nearly choked. 'God, it's like treacle!' she exclaimed with spontaneous candour. 'I thought you said you only took it twice as strong as Connor.'

'Stay put—I'll get the milk,' he laughed as she made to rise.

When he handed it to her Maggie filled her cup to the brim, and still it looked undrinkably black. She toyed with the idea of making herself some tea, then decided that there was a good chance that the coffee would blast her head clear.

'I seem to remember Connor saying something about you being the person he got in to run that London shop, Body and Soul, after Marjorie died,' Slane said, out of the blue.

'He didn't get me to run it,' said Maggie, more than a little thrown. 'In fact, even when his wife was alive I believe it was never a question of anyone running Body and Soul—they all mucked in together, and with great success. Obviously Connor could hardly step in—even apart from all his other commitments he wouldn't have had a clue how the company functioned.'

'Oh, I see—you had?'

'No, I hadn't,' snapped Maggie, now angry. Just who the hell did he think he was, cross-examining her like this? 'I'd just finished my degree and was still at a loose end. I'm sure it can't be difficult for you to imagine how shattered the people were who had worked with her and loved her for so many years. All Connor asked me to do was lend a hand, so I did.'

'What—for two years?' he enquired with undisguised scepticism.

Shaken by how close she was to losing her temper, Maggie rose and went over to the bread bin. Battling to keep a grip on herself, she cut a couple of slices and put them in the toaster. He *did* remember, though clearly he wasn't about to admit it, she told herself angrily, and this snide baiting of her he was indulging in made it plain just how negative and hostile he felt about it all.

'Amazing though it may seem to a high-powered tycoon such as yourself,' she heard herself saying, and had swung round to face him before she realised what she was doing, 'there actually are businesses that operate with everyone happily mucking in and, believe it or not, manage to thrive.

'Body and Soul might only be a natural pharmacy, but they none the less needed someone with the relevant scientific knowledge, so I suppose in that respect I was taking over from Connor's wife.'

He was sitting at the table, his chin propped on his hands, gazing at her as though drinking in her every word.

'My, you sound almost defensive, Maggie,' he drawled. 'I was just being sociable and trying to show some interest.'

'I'm sure you were,' she retorted from between clenched teeth as she turned back to the toaster. 'Would you like some of this toast, or what?'

'I'll have a rummage through the icebox to see if I can reproduce one of Mrs Morrisons's famous fry-ups.'

'There's only bacon and eggs. If you want that I can cook it for you.'

'So can I,' he said, the faint tinge of mockery in his tone setting Maggie's teeth on edge. 'I'll even cook you some too, to prove what a sociable guy I am.'

'That's quite all right—I'll do it,' she said. The last thing she needed was to be standing around with nothing to occupy her. 'You must be tired—what with your body clock being all askew,' she added, just to make sure that he got the message that her cooking him breakfast was not to be the norm. 'Would you like tomatoes with it?'

'I'd love tomatoes with it,' he replied, further irritating her with his mocking stress on her English pronunciation. 'Do you enjoy cooking, Maggie?'

'Not particularly.'

'So, you're just an old-fashioned girl who likes to take care of a man... I think I'm going to enjoy this stay after all.'

'My other reason for offering to cook this is simply that I'm not at my best first thing in the morning,' retorted Maggie, having extreme difficulty in keeping her tone in any way civil. 'I like to have something to keep me occupied, otherwise I'm quite likely to doze off.' She unwrapped the bacon, unable to believe the rubbish she had just spouted. 'And that wouldn't be very sociable, would it?'

'I'll have to take you at your word about how you feel at this hour,' he murmured, 'but from where I'm sitting you look great. You haven't drunk your coffee... I'll make you some fresh.'

There was absolutely no need for him to lean over and against her as he reached for the kettle, but that was what he did. Her body responded in a way that both startled and horrified her, melting to a liquid state of unequivocal sexual excitement as the heady, newly bathed masculine scent of him engulfed her.

So unnerved was she by the totality of that involuntary response that an equally involuntary shriek exploded from her as, in her panic to escape, she leapt smack into the kettle he had just lifted.

'Now, that wasn't very smart, was it?' he drawled, putting down the kettle and taking her face in his hands.

'What are you doing?' she protested, twisting violently in an attempt to escape those hands. 'Stop it!'

'For God's sake, stop being so damned stupid!' he exclaimed, his hands tightening in a vice-like grip. 'Your nose is bleeding.'

'Get your hands off me!' she cried, a note of hysteria slicing through the words as her hands tugged frantically at his arms.

'Hell, anyone walking in here and seeing you dripping blood and freaking out all over the place would assume I was trying to kill you!' he exploded, his eyes blazing fury as he abruptly released her. 'Just what in hell are you playing at?'

'What do you mean, what am *I* playing at?' shrieked Maggie, unable to exert any control over herself. '*You're* the one who's just broken my nose with the kettle!'

'I don't believe this,' he groaned softly to himself, then reached over to a roll of kitchen paper and tore off a couple of sheets. 'Here—dab your nose with that. And for God's sake don't blow it.'

Maggie took the wad of paper and gingerly did as he'd said, the madness at last mercifully subsiding in her. Then she wondered just how much of a mercy it was as she found herself face to face with a blackly scowling man, the angry heave of whose chest had loosened his robe and exposed an expanse of fine, silkily hirsute darkness.

It was when her mind's eye began casually stripping the entire robe from that magnificent body that she was reduced to considering pinching herself to end what had to be a ghastly nightmare.

'It doesn't seem to be bleeding any more,' he muttered, flashing her a distinctly hostile look before grabbing a teatowel and walking over to the fridge. 'You'd better pack this around it for a while,' he said, handing her the towel, now wrapped around a mound of ice-cubes. 'It might prevent it swelling.'

Now feeling an utter fool, Maggie moved towards the cooker, the lumpy towel clamped to her nose.

'Now what are you doing?' he demanded in weary exasperation.

'Cooking your breakfast.'

'Don't you think you have enough to occupy you?' he drawled, shaking his head in disbelief. 'Forget it— we'll go have a look at the lab facilities, then get ourselves breakfast downtown. . .assuming, that is, you're up to it.'

At first Maggie was surprised at how well Slane knew his way around, then she remembered that he had spent quite a bit of time in Dublin.

'Did you come here on holiday regularly?' she asked after a silent battle with herself. They had exchanged barely a word since getting into Connor's car, but a subconscious fatalism in her reasoned that, having committed herself to stay, her best bet was to try to establish at least a veneer of civility between them before she got around to confronting him. The only alternative appeared to be a descent into out-and-out war...

Besides, there was this growing, insistent part of her showing an insatiable need to find out everything there was to know about him... Not that she had any intention of indulging it to the full.

'Not on holiday, exactly,' he replied. 'We did visit quite a bit, but my dad had this thing about me not missing out on the Irish half of me. I went to school here as a kid—though I went through high school in the States. I was also here at Trinity before going on to Yale.'

'Didn't you mind?' exclaimed Maggie involuntarily.

'What was there to mind?'

'Surely it must have been disruptive—switching between the Irish and American education system like that? And what about leaving your family and friends?'

'I was a bright kid, so the differences didn't bother me,' he replied. 'I guess I was also a pretty secure one. It wasn't as though I was packed off to Ireland against my will; I was given the choice and I couldn't wait to live here for a while. As for family and friends, I knew they'd still be there when I got back—which was most vacations.'

Bright, well-adjusted and utterly modest, thought Maggie wryly, and that had just been the child!

'I guess you had a more conventional childhood,' he murmured as, with the outskirts of Dublin behind them, he speeded up along the coastal road, beside which angry grey seas sent foam-tipped waves hurtling across mile after empty mile of pale gold sand.

'I guess you could say that,' responded Maggie drily.

'Oh, I see,' he chuckled, the sound sending shock

waves of heat rippling through her. 'This is to be a "tell all" for me and a "tell nothing" for you. Great.'

Maggie bit back an angry retort, reasoning with herself that she could hardly blame him for the effect he was having on her—an effect of which he seemed, thank heavens, mercifully unaware.

'I'm sorry if you got that impression,' she said, trying so hard to feign normality that she ended up sounding prissy, 'but there really is nothing to tell. I went from one school to the next, in the same town, then on to university—there's hardly anything exotic about that. . . Where exactly are we heading?'

'To a place just outside Dun Laoghaire,' he replied, taking a sudden right turn from the coast road. 'In fact, we'll soon be there.'

Maggie frowned in puzzlement as with each turn they took they drove deeper and deeper into what was obviously a most affluent residential area. 'We are on our way to a laboratory, aren't we?' she muttered, peering out through the rain-bleared windows at houses that were getting grander and sparser by the minute.

'We sure are,' he replied, with a soft laugh, as they entered what was more of a lane than a road, at the end of which stood huge, wrought-iron gates set into a massive, creeper-clad wall. He stopped the car in front of the gates, released his seat belt and opened his door. 'Your turn to drive.'

Before Maggie could utter a word he was out and drawing aside the heavy, creaking gates.

He motioned her to remain where she was once she had driven through, and got in beside her, spraying her with droplets of rain as he shook his glossy dark head like a boisterous puppy.

'Straight on up,' he directed.

It was like driving through a miniature forest, and then a house loomed into view.

'This looks more like a minor stately home than a laboratory site!' exclaimed Maggie as they neared the impressive, ivy-clad building. 'Who on earth owns it?'

'Maurice Ryan—an old friend of my father's,' replied Slane. 'Just follow the drive round to the back of the house and on down to that line of trees—you'll see where to turn once we're there. Maurice is a character and a half, but unfortunately we won't see him—he's off picking daisies at the end of some rainbow or other.'

'He's what?' exclaimed Maggie, following the curve of the drive and bringing the car to a halt in front of a white, single-storey building, hidden from view by the trees behind which it stood.

'Maurice is a botanist. He eats, sleeps and breaths botany. Fortunately he has vast independent means with which to indulge his passion.'

'I take it he's the one who's grown this plant you're going to test?' said Maggie.

Slane nodded. 'Yes, he— Ah, that must be John,' he said as a man clad in waterproofs and wellington boots appeared from around the side of the building. 'You might just as well stay here in the dry while I have a word with him about setting things up for the morning.'

He got out of the car and approached him, and a while later the two of them disappeared inside the building. In less than five minutes they reappeared and stood deep in conversation, the other man every now and then pointing towards a row of greenhouses of varying sizes and shapes and sometimes to the land beyond.

What am I doing here, and with this of all men? Maggie asked herself incredulously as a shiver that was entirely unrelated to the bleakness of the late November weather shuddered through her.

She busied herself for a while, moving back to the passenger seat, but, with that little distraction over, her eyes were drawn back to the taller of the two figures. Whatever it was his shorter companion had said, Slane suddenly threw back his head and laughed, oblivious of the rain now deluging down on them.

That ruinously expensive-looking coat of his would be soaked, thought Maggie; then she found herself smiling at her own innate practicality—after all, what was the odd cashmere coat or two to the seriously wealthy? And Slane Fitzpatrick, apart from everything else he had going for him, was very seriously wealthy.

He slapped the man on the shoulder, then turned and walked back to the car. He was walking to the passenger side, then stopped, gave a lopsided grin, and changed direction.

He's also a very seriously attractive man, thought Maggie as her heart gave a drunken lurch, and I've got to get my act together before I make a complete and utter fool of myself.

'How can you do this to me, Maggie?' he groaned, laughing as he got back into the car. 'I have enough problems with which side of the car to get into in this country without you complicating matters by switching seats on me.'

'Sorry,' she said, her pulse rate still chaotic, 'but it's better if you drive as I'd never find my way—' She broke off with a gasp at the sight of him. 'Have you any idea of the state you're in? Your coat's soaking—and as for your hair. . .!'

He made a soft growling sound in his throat as he turned towards her with a wicked grin, then shook his head vigorously. With a yell of protest Maggie grabbed a box of tissues from the door pocket and flung a handful at him.

'Any intelligent person would have done his talking inside,' she protested.

'Gee, sorry, Mom,' he replied, with an idiot grin, scrunching up the tissues and rubbing his hair with them. 'Oh, great!' he exclaimed in indignant disgust an instant later when the tissues began disintegrating and peppering his hair like soaked confetti. 'This is all your fault,' he complained, running tissue-smeared fingers impatiently through his hair and making matters worse, 'so you can get it out—every last scrap of it!'

'The intention was that you should dry your face with them, not smear them all over your hair,' laughed Maggie as he lowered his head and leaned towards her.

She began removing the clumps of sodden tissue, but as her fingers delved into the thickness of his soaked hair her mind hurtled her back to another time, when it had been the exertions of passion that had dampened the hair in which her fingers had feverishly explored— a passion that had dewed their entwined, naked bodies with its own sultry rain. She snatched back her hand as though scalded, her entire body tensing as it shrank towards the door.

'I—Y-you really ought to get out of that coat,' she stammered when he lifted his head a little to gaze up at her with coolly mocking eyes.

'Ought I?' he drawled, his mouth curving into a smile tinged with mocking malevolence as he straightened. 'We'll go find somewhere to eat... I can get out of it there,' he announced with sudden briskness and started the car.

Maggie gave inordinate attention to fastening her

seat belt, racking her brains for something to say that would miraculously clear the air of the almost palpable tension fogging it.

'I wasn't exactly needed on this trip, was I?' she muttered, and realised that those were hardly the words to produce any miracle. 'I'll do the gates,' she offered when, having made no response, he halted the car before them.

'What, to justify your coming along?' he drawled, opening his door. 'There's no point us both getting wet so I'll do them. It's best if I drive through as well—the seat's probably all messed up too.'

The leather upholstry was wet, Maggie conceded to herself as they went through the tortuous procedure of negotiating the gates, but she could easily have wiped it dry.

'John's got it all in hand for us to start tomorrow,' he said once they were on their way. 'He's been with Maurice God knows how many years. Maurice swears John has forgotten more than the average botanist learns in a lifetime about plants—exotic or otherwise.'

'Does he usually accompany Maurice on field trips?' asked Maggie, welcoming the distraction of the topic with limp relief.

'No,' chuckled Slane. 'It seems Maurice has never been able to persuade John to set foot on a plane, so John and the team run everything while he's off gadding about.'

'You must have been pleased to hear they'd managed to grow this plant. How near to extinction is it?'

'Extremely near—in its natural habitat, that is,' he replied as he eased the car into the city's rush-hour traffic. 'It grows like a weed just about anywhere. The trouble is it mututes and ends up lacking the vital

properties that made it of interest in the first place.' He
swung the car into the entrance of a multi-storey car
park. 'I've just realised,' he muttered, turning to her
once they were parked, 'I don't have any change on
me—how about you?'

Maggie rummaged in her bag. She took out her
purse, and a comb which she handed to him.

'I'll get a ticket while you get the rest of that tissue
out of your hair.'

That she was accompanied by the sort of man who
turned heads was made abundantly clear to Maggie as
they made their way from the car park towards Grafton
Street. She found herself trying to remember what her
own reaction had been in that very first instant when
she had laid eyes on Slane, but her uncooperative mind
kept leaping too far forward, presenting her with
images that made her cheeks burn despite the chill of
the rain now drizzling lightly against them.

'We're going to one of my old haunts—Bewleys,' he
told her, the touch of his hand at her elbow light as he
guided her through a sudden swell of people.

'I've never seen so many people!' exclaimed Maggie.
'Is it always this crowded?'

'I guess quite a few of these people are on their way
to work,' he laughed, steering her through a doorway
and into a shop heavily scented with the aroma of
coffee, 'but Grafton Street is usually pretty lively.'

Slane at last removed his coat as they entered the
famous coffee-house, grinning at Maggie's reaction of
wide-eyed delight as she gazed around the dark wood
and marble interior, packed almost to the hilt, and
filled with the soft buzz of conversation.

'Are you hungry?' he asked once they were seated.

'Starving,' she replied, a hand rising self-consciously
to her damp hair as her eyes met those of a strikingly
attractive woman at the next table who had just finished
giving Slane a thorough perusal. The woman smiled in
sympathy and patted her own hair as much as to say,
Mine too, then resumed conversation with her
companion.

Just about every woman in their immediate vicinity
had done it, observed Maggie without rancour—given
Slane an appreciative inspection, followed by a quick
appraisal of the woman accompanying such an Adonis.
A pretty natural reaction, she thought with a tinge of
ruefulness that quickly deteriorated into a pang of
alarm as her nose began to throb—with her present
luck it was probably shining like a beacon!

'Shall I just order us the full works?' asked Slane as
a waitress approached.

Maggie nodded, and made the grave error of distract-
ing herself from gloomy speculation regarding her
appearance by subjecting Slane to a surreptitious
inspection as he spoke to the waitress.

All right, so she was still in a state of shock, she
reasoned miserably, feeling as if her mind was operating on badly depleted batteries as her eyes lapped him
up. But she had to snap out of it, she told herself
angrily. And accepting one minute that her past was a
fact that she could no longer avoid facing, then in the
next wallowing in the fantasy that she would wake to
find it had all been a terrible dream was only a short
cut to insanity.

'You look pensive,' Slane observed when the waitress had left, his eyes disconcertingly inscrutable as
they flickered over her.

'Do I?' she exclaimed with a guilty start.

'Yes.' He leaned back in his chair, his amused, mocking eyes holding hers.

'Well, I was thinking,' she blurted out defensively, and then had to ransack her mind for a topic to back up the claim. 'I was thinking...about that plant. Obviously the aim is to reproduce it intact—but if it grows like a weed why get Maurice to do the trials here? Surely it would have been more practical for you to get someone to grow it in America?'

'Perhaps—except that I didn't get anyone to grow it for me anywhere,' he replied unenlighteningly, then began gazing around him, a look of bored detachment on his face.

Maggie felt anger and confusion doing battle within her. Even if she had only been roped in at the last moment as a lowly lab assistant, it was perfectly natural for her to show an interest in the project... Or perhaps it was simply that he was loath to discuss anything with a woman with whom he had had a one-night stand and whom he was determined not to acknowledge.

'Ah!' he exclaimed, his face brightening. 'Food. What a welcome sight.'

What a welcome distraction, thought Maggie, gratefully inhaling the glorious aromas emanating from the huge platters set before them. Whether he remembered her or whether he was simply an uncommunicative boor with a bad memory, for now she didn't give a toss—she was starving!

They ate in the silence that such hearty, immaculately prepared food warranted. And it was only after her hunger pangs had been well and truly pandered to that Maggie found her thoughts straying back to where they had been before the arrival of the food had rescued her.

'I feel it's almost criminal to leave all this,' she sighed, resisting the tug of those thoughts, 'but I couldn't manage another mouthful—there was enough for three on my plate.'

He grinned across at her, then casually speared a juicily glistening sausage from her plate with his fork.

'It's just as well Mrs Morrison isn't around,' he laughed. 'I once made the near-fatal error of telling her I'd breakfasted here—boy, did I have to grovel to get back into her good books.' He demolished the sausage, then returned to her plate to forage further.

It was what lovers did, thought Maggie weakly—ate titbits from one another's plates... And wasn't that what they had been so briefly—the most passionate of lovers?

'So, this Maurice doesn't actually work for your company,' she stated, her need for distraction driving her back to the topic he had so abruptly dismissed.

'Maurice?' he echoed, one blue-black eyebrow arching superciliously. 'I thought I'd already explained—Maurice doesn't work for anyone. He's just a brilliant botanist who does his own thing.'

It was like pulling teeth, thought Maggie angrily. 'You haven't explained anything—despite your intimation last night that you would,' she snapped. 'And that's why I'm still asking.'

'So what do you want to know?' he drawled, his eyes like glittering ice.

'Well, for a start, if this is Maurice's thing, why can't he do his own analyses?'

'It isn't his thing.'

'Well, thanks a million,' hissed Maggie across the table at him. 'If that's the way you motivate your staff, all I can say is God help them!'

'You need motivating to assist with a bit of lab work, do you?' he enquired, scowling back at her.

'Forget I ever showed any interest,' she snapped, picking up her coffee-cup and draining it. 'And we can do the work in complete silence for all I care.'

His lips were pursed as he picked up the coffee-pot and refilled both their cups. 'Give me a break, Maggie,' he muttered. 'I've been through so many time zones in the past few days that right now I'm not too sure which way is up.'

He ladled sugar into his coffee and stirred it, a closed, far-away expression on his face. 'I've no idea whether or not Maurice has succeeded in reproducing this plant in its pristine state, but we'll know soon enough after it's been tested—'

He broke off to take some coffee, an expression of utter bleakness on his face. 'Maurice and my father go back a long way... They first met as kids and kept in regular touch, both being prolific letter writers, right up until my father's death.'

His father, thought Maggie, her heart constricting.

'Slane, I—I...' she stammered, guilt flooding her. 'Look, if you'd rather not talk about it—'

'Make up your mind,' he cut in exasperatedly. 'Do you want to hear about this or not?'

'I want to hear,' she replied robotically. She had known from the little that Connor had said that Slane bore wounds with which she was achingly familiar... Now his had been opened up and there was nothing that could be done to spare him.

'It seems Maurice came across this plant a few years ago and wrote to my father about it. Some forest tribe or other used it medicinally—mainly as an antidote to poisons and allergies. Maurice plainly thought it was worth investigating—'

He broke off to ask a passing waitress for the bill. 'A while back Maurice got in touch with me. Off and on, since my father's death, he'd been experimenting with a range of different growing media. And now he's come up with several plants he feels are worth testing.'

'He must be so nervous now that they're about to be tested,' said Maggie as the waitress returned with the bill.

'I doubt if he'll give it too much thought until he gets the results,' said Slane, his tone amused. 'Oh, he'll keep at it if he hasn't succeeded—but that's Maurice. Give him a botanical problem to puzzle over and he'll happily spend the next decade or so solving it—or proving there is no solution.'

'Do you think there's a chance he has solved it?' asked Maggie as they both rose.

He shrugged. 'Who knows?' His eyes caught hers before sweeping slowly down the length of her body; then they swept back up again to linger finally on her parted lips and take in the hectic warmth that his deliberations had brought to her cheeks.

When his eyes at last returned to hers they were filled with mocking challenge. 'Who knows what we're about to discover once we get started?'

CHAPTER THREE

THEIR conversation in the famous coffee-house had unsettled them both.

It had left Maggie in a mood of dark reflection, in which she found herself digging deeper into the store of banished memories already disturbed by Slane's arrival. Slane it had left edgy and cynical one moment, then mockingly salacious the next, as those heavy-lidded eyes would catch hers and appear to make suggestions that bore no relation to the innocuous words he happened to be uttering.

Whatever the memories it had stirred in him, as far as Maggie was concerned it was having the effect of accentuating every negative quality he possessed.

So far she hadn't retaliated, restrained by too many memories of how appalling her own behaviour had been as she had struggled to come to terms with the devastation of grief.

'Connor mentioned that you'd decided to become a teacher,' stated Slane as the car ground to a halt in yet another hold-up in the traffic. 'How come?'

Maggie mentally braced herself; he had spoken the words, but there hadn't been any trace of interest in them.

'I decided it was time I had a proper career. . .and my father taught.'

'What subject did he teach?'

'Chemistry.'

Now they were on decidedly dodgy ground, thought

Maggie, her entire body tensing. Just one snide remark from him in relation to her father and that would be it as far as her feelings of empathy were concerned.

'I hope you hadn't anything planned for today,' he muttered as the line of traffic crawled forward a few feet before stopping again. 'Who knows? We could be stuck here till dark. Now wouldn't that be fun?'

Maggie made the error of glancing at him and again found herself bathed in what could only be described as a come-to-bed look—albeit a decidedly mocking one.

'Why do you keep doing that?' she exploded, goaded beyond restraint.

'Doing what?'

'Looking at me like that!'

'And what way is that?'

Maggie clamped her mouth tightly shut. Well, at least that was her guilt trip over, she told herself angrily, and a totally misplaced one it had been too. The man was probably incapable of the finer feelings with which she had so foolishly been crediting him—he was a complete and utter boor!

'I guess this disorientation I'm suffering—'

'Spare me the drivel,' pleaded Maggie witheringly.

'Has stripped away my inhibitions,' he continued unconcernedly. 'Thank God for that!' he exclaimed as the traffic at last flowed freely. 'I can't be the first guy who's looked at you appreciatively—you're a very beautiful woman, Maggie.'

'I'm a moderately attractive woman,' she snapped. 'So I suggest you save your breath.' Which was exactly what she should be doing, she told herself exasperatedly.

'They say beauty is in the eye of the beholder,' he

murmured, his tone all sweetness and reason, 'and mine reckons you're beautiful. I mean, what is there that could be improved on? You have eyes that—'

'Shut up!' howled Maggie, something in her snapping completely. 'Just stop it!'

'Now there's an enigma for you—a woman who throws a fit when a man tells her she's beautiful. I wonder what your problem is, Maggie?'

'I'm *not* throwing a fit!' Horrified by the hysteria shrilling her tone, she fought to contain herself. 'And I don't have a problem—unless it's that I've put up with your snide remarks and. . .and everything else you've been dishing out to me! And, while we're on the subject of problems, if you have one over working with me just say so and I can get the next flight home.'

'As you well know, I can't afford to have a problem with it—you're all I've got.'

'Forgive me for saying so, but it takes a lot of believing that someone of your reputation would have such a problem replacing me,' retorted Maggie, his lack of denial about his behaviour stirring up another seething swarm of does-he-or-doesn't-he-remember-mes in her beleaguered mind.

'And what do you know of my reputation, Maggie?' he drawled as he swung the car into the drive of the house. 'It would be a laboratory assistant I'd be replacing, not someone to warm my bed.'

'You're disgusting,' gasped Maggie, her hands shaking uncontrollably as they fumbled to release her seat belt.

'Disgusting?' he enquired softly, his hand covering hers and stilling its frantic scrabbling.

'You know perfectly well I was referring to your professional reputation, not to you. . .to your—' She broke off, praying for a bottomless pit to appear for her to throw herself into.

'What—are you too prudish even to say it?' he asked in that same, steely soft voice. 'My reputation with women?'

'I'm *not* a prude!' she howled, tearing her hand free.

'So how come you're giving such a good impression of being one?' he enquired, releasing her seat belt.

'And what, exactly, is your definition of one?' she demanded, fury rampaging through her. 'Ice maiden', 'prude'—Peter had progressed to other synonyms the night they had parted; vicious and vulgarly explicit, he had hurled them all at her fleeing figure. 'Any woman who doesn't fling herself into your arms?' Dear God, what was she saying? 'Any woman who doesn't worship at the shrine of your looks and power?'

Well, at least his power hadn't come into it with her, she consoled herself desolately as she leapt from the car.

'Any woman who does either of those things is the ultimate turn-off as far as I'm concerned,' he informed her silkily, appearing as though by magic beside her.

She looked up into his scowling face, a feeling of overwhelming weariness creeping over her.

'And, since you ask, my definition of a prude,' he ground out before she had a chance to utter a word, 'is one who, among other things, finds a humorous reference to anything remotely sexual disgusting. OK, so it wasn't rib-tickingly funny, but it wasn't disgusting.

'I'd also have said that any woman who jumps a foot in the air any time a guy happens to brush next to her might also fit the description—though I agree that's debatable. But as I'm a fairly honest guy I have to admit that I didn't exactly go out of my way to avoid brushing against you last night. . .

'I guess it's down to my over-inflated ego that I didn't get the obvious message—that you simply find me physically repulsive.'

It was such a ludicrous statement that Maggie gave an incredulous laugh.

'You find that funny?' he enquired, reaching out and taking her by the shoulders.

Her laughter was replaced by a sharp exclamation of protest the instant he touched her. When she angrily began trying to twist herself free his grasp on her tightened.

'For God's sake, what do you think I'm about to do—ravish you in broad daylight?' he demanded furiously. 'Why can't we just handle this civilly?'

'Handle what civilly?' demanded Maggie, her body rigid beneath his hands still on her shoulders.

'The fact that I'm so attracted to you and you find me repulsive. That doesn't mean—'

'Why do you keep saying I find you repulsive?' she burst out, stunned by his casual claim to attraction.

'Because when a guy starts putting out feelers towards a woman he finds attractive there are subtle ways she can brush him off and still remain on friendly terms with him. But when a woman feels repelled by—'

'I *don't* feel repelled!' she yelled at him, her head reeling. 'Neither do I find you repulsive. How many times do you need to be told? And as for your putting out feelers of any description—don't make me laugh!'

'I'd rather you laughed than. . . Oh, to hell with this!' he muttered savagely, jerking her into his arms.

Had she been capable of reasoning, Maggie might have come up with shock or possibly even a brainstorm as the explanation for what happened next. No longer was she standing in the fine drizzle of a bleak November day; she had simply woken from what felt like a long sleep and was back in the arms of her lover.

Before, when she had catnapped in his arms, she had awoken to an instant hunger. Now it was as though it had been the hunger itself that had awoken her, gnawing relentlessly within her as her mouth responded uninhibitedly to the bruising ardour raining down on it.

Before, it hadn't been just her mouth that his lips and tongue had explored with such devastating thoroughness... And, before, their bodies had been free, not hidden from touch beneath this infuriating swaddle of clothing.

Her hands moved impatiently against the material of his coat, hesitating as the dampness they encountered triggered the memory of rain. Then it was the rain she felt—a gentle, almost caressing wetness on her upturned face.

Yet even as reality was returning to her her every instinct was to push it away. The passionately exploring mouth to which her own still clung had driven her body to a point from which there had been no turning back before, and now her body felt no inclination whatever to be turned back.

'Please, please, please,' she chanted in breathless incoherence against the lips from which she was now forcing her own away. 'I'm sorry... Please don't do this to me.'

'Why should you be sorry?' he muttered, his chest heaving and a look of dazed incredulity on his face as he released her. 'I was the one who was wrong.'

Unable to speak, she gazed up at him with a look of complete bemusement.

'I was very wrong—you don't find me repulsive.'

Had there been amusement, open sarcasm, anything at all in his tone, she would at least have had some idea of what was going on behind those narrowed, enigmatic eyes. But it was the utter flatness with which he had delivered those words that filled her with a sickening sense of hopelessness.

'Do you need the car?' he asked abruptly.

Still not capable of speech, Maggie shook her head.

'Right. I have things to do,' he stated, walking round to the driver's side and opening the door. 'I have my own keys, so don't bother waiting up for me.'

It was late by the time Maggie got into bed and Slane still hadn't returned. Not that she gave a toss, she told herself as she switched off the bedside light and snuggled under the bedclothes.

She had put off going to bed for as long as she possibly could. She had washed and done a load of ironing and then she had bathed, staying in the bath so long that twice she had had to let some of the cooling water out to top it up with hot.

In many ways, all she had been doing was postponing the inevitable moment when she would be lying here in the darkened silence, she thought edgily, but at least she had come to terms with the fact that there could be no rushing the process that had begun in her—just as there could be no stopping it.

But already the darkness was filling her with doubt. What could she possibly sort out with so many imponderables clouding every issue?

She turned over onto her side and and forced herself to answer her own question. For a start, there was to be no more of this does-he-doesn't-he nonsense. If he did... OK, it didn't pay to go into that, she conceded miserably, but she had no intention of subjecting herself to any more of these nerve-racking guessing games.

She flopped over onto her stomach, burying her face in the pillow as the memories broke free.

Whatever he was now, Slane hadn't been the villain then, even if his saving of her had turned out to be such a double-edged sword. The villain had always been Peter... If it hadn't been for Peter she would never have reacted as she had to Slane calling her a prude.

Almost from the start Peter had made references to what he'd described as her strait-laced attitude towards sex, his remarks always cloaked in terms of amused indulgence. But there had been no sign of that amused indulgence that night when she had finally given herself to him.

She shuddered, burying her face deeper into the pillow as she remembered the naïvety with which she had decided that the time had come, and the same carefree innocence with which she had demanded that the setting be somewhere opulent and special. Peter had chosen the venue, made all the arrangements and whisked her off to their fairy-tale destination.

Perhaps, in her heart of hearts, she had hoped for Paris, but the Georgian splendour of Brighton hadn't disappointed her. But Peter's insensitive dismissal of the apprehensions that had begun stirring within her, his callous lack of patience with her innocence, had rendered him a brutal stranger and what she had naïvely dreamed would be a fairy tale a harrowing nightmare.

She stuffed her fist in her mouth as huge sobs began racking her.

'You've got to learn to relax,' he had informed her irritably once the mercifully brief physical phase of her nightmare was over. 'And with your attitudes you should have realised it would be completely unrealistic to expect to enjoy the first time.'

It was then that the unfeeling monster whom she could no longer delude herself she loved had tried to drag her back into his loathsome arms, and then that she had broken free, grabbing her things and locking herself in the bathroom.

Under the shower she had scrubbed herself raw; once dressed, she had gathered up the rest of her things and put them in her holdall to the accompaniment of a torrent of vicious abuse. The abuse had still been pouring from him when she had quietly closed the door to hell behind her.

Drained by those memories, but accepting them as a healing step forward, she turned on to her side and fell into a sound sleep.

'Thank God,' exclaimed Slane as he and Maggie followed John into the small ante-room of the laboratory, 'the place is heated!'

'Ah, well,' chuckled John. 'For all his leaping about in jungles, Maurice can't be doing without his creature comforts when he's at home. Mind you, when he does lock himself away in here he doesn't set foot in the house all day, so he has everything laid on for himself down here.'

He pulled the door closed, shutting out the icy blast it had been letting in.'That's better. Now, I'll just be showing you where everything is.'

Maggie could hardly believe her eyes—the small chamber was a veritable Aladdin's cave, everything stored neatly out of sight behind cupboard doors. There was a cupboard in which to store their outer clothing, another containing lab wear—all of it disposable. Behind one set of doors were cloakroom facilities and behind another was what amounted almost to a miniature kitchen. . . And that was just the ante-room, she thought in amazement.

'I'll not come into the lab itself,' John informed them, his bright blue eyes twinkling in his weather-beaten face. 'I've already been through the palaver of stripping down this morning, but I'm sure you two scientists don't need any showing around anyway.'

'I'm sure we don't,' laughed Slane, and pulled a friendly face at Maggie. 'You just keep us supplied with the plants, and we'll keep our noses to the grindstone.'

'Yes—well, I've left you your first batch in there, ready prepared.' John smiled. 'Maurice says you'll probably be needing two days to work on a batch, but if you find that's too long or not enough just let me know. Right—I'll be leaving you to it.'

The laboratory area itself was designed and equipped to a level that took Maggie's breath away. All in all, this compact little building had probably cost a good deal more than an average-sized house, she reckoned with incredulity.

'Quite the rich man's toy, isn't it?' murmured Slane, reading her mind. 'Though I guess the botanical fraternity wouldn't agree.'

'I thought botanists worked in greenhouses,' said Maggie. 'Not that I'm complaining,' she added hastily. 'This is fantastic.'

She had entered the kitchen that morning, weak with trepidation, to be greeted with an almost formally polite offer of tea and a boiled egg. They had breakfasted together much as two strangers obliged to share the same table in a hotel dining room might have — exchanging the occasional impersonal pleasantry.

'I'll just get these ready and then I'll give you a run-down on how we'll go about things,' he said, opening up drawers and cabinets and selecting instruments and equipment as though utterly at home in his surroundings.

Maggie watched as he lined everything up meticulously. She knew practically every inch of his body, she thought with an almost detached amazement, but she didn't know *him* at all. And this morning at breakfast, as they'd exchanged their stilted pleasantries, she had almost been tempted to believe that yesterday had never happened.

'Right — let's just go through the routine we'll be following,' he said, drawing out a stool for her to sit on. 'But first I'd better let you in on the bad news.'

Maggie's look of alarm brought a soft chuckle from him — a response which alarmed her even further as it started up a softly melting churning sensation in the pit of her stomach.

'It's only that I have to warn you, in case Connor hasn't already, that on a scale of one to ten for boring and repetitive work this would probably rate twelve —' He broke off and grinned apologetically. 'And I'm afraid with this baby we're working with a zero margin of error — we just don't have any leeway.'

Since the moment they had first entered the compact building there had been a subtle yet noticeable change in him.

The look he had flashed her in the ante-room had been spontaneous, friendly — the sort of look one bestowed on an ally. And now there was no mistaking the enthusiasm in his voice as he outlined the routine they would be following—an enthusiasm that, considering the position he held and the relative lowliness of the task involved, she should have been finding slightly incongruous—except that she wasn't.

He was right—the work was repetitive and painstaking almost to the extreme of being finicky, but at no point during the hours that sped by, relieved only by the cups of coffee that whichever of them had a spare moment would slip out to make, did Maggie find it in the least boring.

Lost in their shared time warp, they both started at the sound of knocking on the lab door.

'Are you two still in the land of the living?' demanded John's jocular voice. 'It's gone seven.'

The look on Slane's face before he went to the lab door and then stepped through it to have a word with the Irishman confirmed Maggie's own thoughts— John's sense of humour was somewhat on the obscure side. But when she glanced down at her watch to find out exactly what the time was she gave a gasp of disbelief.

'Hell, I don't believe this,' Slane was muttering when he returned. 'Just sling those in the autoclave while I store this lot... For God's sake, Maggie, why didn't you say something?'

'What, for instance?' she retorted sharply. It was bad enough feeling as though she had just been dragged from a deep sleep, but worse finding herself being addressed in such a hectoring tone. So much for the apparent camaraderie between them, she thought resentfully as she sealed the autoclave and switched it on; it hadn't even lasted out the clearing-up stage.

'You must have noticed the time,' he stated in that same, almost accusing tone.

'Well, you're wrong,' she retorted, marching out into the ante-room and shedding her lab coat.

'What I meant was that I didn't intend us to work such crazy hours,' he said, following her. 'What do we do with these?' he demanded, holding up the lab coat he had just shrugged out of.

Maggie took it and placed them both in the receptacle provided.

'Just because I get carried away it doesn't mean you have to,' he persisted, handing her her coat and getting into his own. 'You have to speak up for yourself, otherwise—'

'I'm perfectly capable of speaking up for myself,' she snapped, opening the outer door and stepping out into what felt like Siberia. 'And, anyway, I've a feeling that's the only way my brain would have absorbed and stored all those fiddly preparations—simply by keeping going once I'd got started. Quite honestly, had we stopped for lunch I'm sure it would have taken me ages to get back into the swing of what we'd been doing again.'

'So you feel you've absorbed and stored enough to follow those routines tomorrow, do you?' he asked, arriving at the car almost on her heels.

'I might need a bit of prompting here and there,' she replied, flashing him a wary look—if he was going to start being snide she was in no mood to take it quietly. 'But, on the whole, yes.'

'Good,' he stated, unlocking the car doors. 'Because going without food all day doesn't agree with me. Tomorrow I shall expect you to remind me when it's lunchtime.'

If that was his idea of a joke, thought Maggie irritably as she got into the car, his tone wasn't giving it away.

'Hang on a minute!' she exclaimed as he started up the engine. 'I'll drive to the gates.' And save all that ridiculous palaver of his leaping in and out of the car that they'd gone through again that morning, she added silently—did he think she wasn't capable of opening a couple of gates?

'No need,' he replied, driving off. 'John's expecting a consignment of compost so he's left them open. I forgot to ask—is there any food in the house for tonight?'

'According to Connor, the freezer's full—'

'The freezer?' he exclaimed exasperatedly. 'He doesn't have a microwave cooker—I'll be dead before anything defrosts. We'd better eat out.'

'I was going to add, before you started having a fit,' said Maggie with equal exasperation, 'that there's also one of Mrs Morrisons' goulashes in the fridge.'

'Thank goodness for that,' muttered Slane.

As long as he didn't expect her to prepare it, thought Maggie mutinously, by now feeling utterly exhausted yet ravenously hungry.

'However, I'll see to the food,' he announced when they arrived back at the house. 'You go freshen up.'

Maggie was seething with fury as she climbed the stairs. On the face of it, it was very thoughtful of him to get the meal ready while she bathed, but his tone had robbed his words of anything approaching thoughtfulness.

Perhaps, after the other night's little mishap with the vegetables, he thought that she was incapable of putting a meal together. . . And anyone in the least sensitive might have been forgiven for feeling a social outcast on being ordered to freshen up the way she had just been!

She showered rather than having the long soak in a hot bath that she would have preferred, kidding herself that it was because Slane, ravenous as he had claimed to be, would waste no time in getting the meal ready. Deep down she knew that it was because she simply wasn't up to a prolonged period alone with her thoughts.

'I couldn't find any vegetables,' he told her without turning from the potatoes he was mashing when she entered the kitchen.

'I'm sure we won't miss them,' said Maggie, busying herself by laying the table. 'The goulash smells wonderful.' The delicious aroma assailing her nostrils had begun reminding her with a vengeance of how long ago it was since she had last eaten.

'I thought I'd better heat it on top of the cooker,' he muttered, taking the lid off a heavy enamelled casserole dish and prodding its contents, 'just to make sure it's safely heated through.'

He took his food very seriously, thought Maggie with an involuntary stab of amusement, and, judging by the dampness of his hair and the fact that he had changed into a baggy, off-white sweatshirt and jeans, he had also managed to fit in a shower in the midst of his culinary preparations.

The goulash, when they sat down to eat, was cooked through to perfection, and the potatoes, to Maggie's surprise, had been creamed to a matching perfection. With anyone else, she would have made a complimentary comment, but she was too unnerved by the weight of the silence that had developed between them to risk breaking into it.

'This is delicious,' Maggie ventured eventually. 'Mrs Morrison is a wonderful cook.'

He gave a wry smile. 'As I told Connor a few years back—when he was droning on, as he's given to, about my still not being "spoken for", as he puts it—Find me a woman who can cook like Mrs Morrison and I'll marry her if she'll have me.'

'I suppose that's a good enough reason for getting married,' murmured Maggie drily, removing their plates and taking them over to the dishwasher.

'That, and carrying on the line,' he agreed, deadpan.

'But of course,' she muttered, opening the dishwasher and putting in the plates. The awful thing was that he probably meant it, she thought.

'Yeah—a woman who can cook like Mrs Morrison and give me a son. . . What more could I ask of life?'

'What more indeed?' she murmured, slinging in the cutlery with more force than she had intended. Surely he had to be joking? 'It goes without saying that a daughter simply wouldn't do.'

'That's the way my great-grandfather—the founder of the Fitzpatrick empire—decreed it must be: executive control of the business to be handed down to the first son of the first son—or the next male in line.'

'Obviously it doesn't pay to be a female member of the Fitzpatrick family,' observed Maggie a shade tartly as she took a bowl of fruit from the dresser and placed it on the table. Was she really taking part in this bizarre conversation?

'If it's bucks you're talking, it pays very nicely,' he murmured, helping himself to an apple. 'The profits aren't left exclusively to the first in line,' he continued, adding blandly, 'though we do have this tendency to produce mainly males—when we're actually breeding, that is—Connor's sister being the only female Fitzpatrick for several generations.'

'You make it sound like cattle!' she exclaimed, so taken aback that she had actually sat down and taken a pear from the bowl before she realised what she had done. 'What exactly do you mean—when you're actually breeding?'

'Well, no one could accuse me of being prolific,' he replied without any apparent rancour. 'I'm the only one of my generation—my mother wasn't able to have more children after me. My father did have twin brothers, but they died in a sail-boat accident when they were still kids. Connor and Marjorie never got around to having any kids and neither has Maura, his sister.'

Maggie glanced down at the untouched pear on her plate. Though there had been an underlying lightness in his tone the fact that he had chosen to reveal quite so much about his family had left her feeling peculiarly on edge.

'Would you like some tea?' she asked, uncomfortably aware of how abruptly she had terminated the conversation, and resenting the capriciousness with which tiredness and confusion were affecting her mind. 'I'll—'

'Tea?' he cut in, plainly amused. He tilted back his chair, his eyes filled with mocking enquiry as they lazily scrutinised her. 'Maggie, are you trying to tell me something?'

'All I did was offer you tea,' she snapped, caught completely off guard by the swiftness of the change in him. 'If you'd prefer coffee all you have to do is say so.'

'I don't think I'll have either right now,' he murmured, the mockery in his eyes gentling to teasing. 'But as for your offer of tea—when a man virtually admits to a woman that the way to his heart is through his stomach, he could be forgiven for regarding such an offer as something of a put-down.'

'I dare say,' she murmured, her mood switching as quickly as his had. 'But how many women in their right mind would actually want to discover the way to your heart?'

'And there was I, convinced I was a great catch,' he sighed, rolling his eyes heavenwards.

'Perhaps you would be,' said Maggie, deciding that now she was saddled with this exchange she might as well enjoy it, 'for a masochist.'

The threatrical look of pained hurt with which he responded brought her closer to laughter than she would have dreamed possible scant seconds ago.

'Just consider what the poor creature would be in for if she had the misfortune to catch you,' she embroidered sweetly. 'Gourmet meals day in and day out, not to mention that strict breeding programme she'd be on. Tell me, Slane, do the Fitzpatricks still go in for beheading their women if they fail to produce a male heir, or have they managed to drag themselves into this century in that respect?'

'Tut-tut, Maggie,' he murmured, flashing her a startingly wicked look of reproof while rising to his feet. 'Did no one ever tell you it's the male who determines the sex of a child?'

'Oh, yes, but I'd always thought that men like you never quite believed it,' she laughed.

'Perhaps I should start putting you straight about men like me, Maggie,' he said, spreading his hands on the table and leaning across it towards her.

She drew back instantly, a jerky reflex action over which she had no control.

'You're not, as Connor would say, spoken for, are

you, Maggie?' he enquired, his tone reverting to
mockery.

'I... Wh-whether I am or not is no business of
yours,' she stammered weakly, and could have cringed.
No doubt, when she had absolutely no need of it, a
wittily dismissive retort would come leaping to her
mind.

'Miss Prim might not reckon it is,' he murmured in
silky tones, 'but what about Maggie? Or have you
forgotten?'

So this was it, she thought almost detachedly as she
felt everything drain from her.

'Or perhaps I only imagined what happened yesterday,' he continued softly. 'Perhaps I never did hold a
vibrant, passionate woman in my arms—a woman
whose response led me to believe I had at least the
right to ask whether or not she was spoken for.'

'Slane... I... You're not being fair,' she choked, her
mouth so dry that she could barely get the words out.

'Am I not?' he drawled, straightening. 'Well, be
warned, Maggie, that's not about to change...not
unless you can give me a darned good reason for it to.'

CHAPTER FOUR

'BY THE way, Mrs Morrison called early this morning to remind you about the food in the freezer in case Connor had forgotten to,' said Slane as he meticulously recorded details of their last batch of work. 'She nearly had forty fits when I answered the phone,' he added, with a chuckle.

'I'm sure she's sorry to have missed you,' murmured Maggie as she prepared another slide. 'How long has she been with Connor?'

Yesterday had told her that the work itself was unlikely to cause her any problems once she was into the swing of it, just as yesterday had confirmed that the man with whom she was doing the work embodied an insurmountable problem.

Yet this morning, contrary to her every dread, his behaviour towards her had been faultless—no mocking innuendo, no glance or touch from which she might flinch. He seemed thoroughly relaxed, every now and then lightening what so easily could have become the tedium of their work with an uncontentious comment to which she could respond without effort.

'For as long as I can remember,' he replied. 'I know he and Marjorie tried to persuade her to join them when they moved to London, but they might just as well have asked her to camp in the Sahara.

'Her excuse was keeping an eye on their Dublin place while they were away. Connor used to let visiting academics stay there, and folklore has it that until they'd wormed their way into Mrs Morrison's good books she wasn't above checking their feet for dirt before letting them into the house. But Marjorie's death hit her badly. . .as, I guess, it did us all.'

Maggie remembered the stunned reaction of the members of the small, privileged group, of which she had been a member, to the news of the fatal stroke that had robbed their much loved professor of the wife he had so obviously adored.

'I remember the Prof saying that the—' She broke off, realising that those remembered words had related as much to the loss of Slane's father as they had to that of Marjorie.

'That the effects of the terrible suddenness of it on those left behind has to be weighed against an alternative hell—both Marjorie and my father could so easily have been left unbearably maimed,' he finished for her quietly before straightening and glancing down at his watch. 'We need to get some fresh food in; there's practically nothing in the house besides the frozen stuff. If you feel like a break, we could do some shopping now and then take an early lunch.'

'I'd rather plough on through this batch if you don't mind,' said Maggie, cursing herself for her lack of sensitivity; her own father had been gone far longer than his, yet even now a chance remark could catch her off guard and leave her swamped in pain. 'Perhaps you could pick me up a sandwich when you're doing the shopping.'

'A sandwich?' he queried, as though the idea struck him as slightly obscene. 'You should have a proper lunch. I can—'

'I promise you, a sandwich is usually the most I ever

eat for lunch,' she assured him. 'Anything more and my appetite's spoiled for the evening.'

He grumbled a bit but finally left—though not before bringing her in a cup of tea which he plonked down on the counter beside her.

Maggie reached for the cup as the sound of the car disappeared into the distance, her expression one of troubled thought as she held it to her lips. His gesture had touched her, just as his painfully abrupt dropping of the subject that had inadvertently touched on his father's death had.

Her thoughts began straying towards the long sup- pressed memories that had now begun surfacing thick and fast. Part of her still kept resisting them—and little wonder, she concluded wearily. The night he had arrived the devastatingly erotic nature of her random snatches of memory had appalled her, so much so that last night, when her mind had begged to examine those memories in their entirety, the old barriers had gone up.

And boy, had they gone up with a vengeance, she thought wryly as she drank the tea; she had crammed her head with a million distractions until finally she had sunk into an exhausted sleep shortly before dawn.

She gave an exasperated shake of her head as she settled back into her work, barely bothering to steel herself as last night's barriers began tumbling.

Three years ago, the veneer of calm that had settled on her the instant she had closed the door on Peter's vicious tirade had crumbled when the hotel receptionist had told her that there wasn't a train to London until the morning.

'Sorry to butt in, but I couldn't help overhearing.' He had been around her own age—the fair-haired,

dinner-suited young man who had addressed her.
'There's bound to be someone in our party who'll be
able to give you a lift back to London. There won't be
anyone leaving till later, so come and join in the fun...
I'm Tom, by the way.'

Tom's cheery blandishments had drowned her dazed
protests, and seconds later she had found herself in the
midst of a throng of admiring men, and downing
champagne as though it were lemonade.

Of course the champagne had gone to her head, but
not enough to prevent her deducing that she had joined
a stag party, and that all the attention being showered
on her by so many men was down to her being one of
only two or three women present.

Later she had slipped out to the terrace to clear her
head and escape the empty flattery that was now
beginning to irritate rather than salve her shattered
self-esteem.

Maggie paused in her work, the ghost of an exasperated laugh escaping her. Even now she was resisting
it—the memory of her first sight of Slane Fitzpatrick.

But then he had been the stranger—a tall, dark
silhouette gazing out into the night. He had turned
towards her at the soft sound of her tread, and the light
from behind him had caught his face. In that instant,
knowing nothing of him, she had found herself compar-
ing him with the other forty or so men still inside. Like
children trying to score points against one another they
had vied for her attention...

Yes, even in that first instant she had instinctively
known that this was a man who had never felt the need
to indulge in such puerile games.

'Do me a favour,' he had said in that soft American

voice of his, 'and tell whoever sent you that I've gone to bed.'

Her hands now hesitated momentarily in their task as amazement filled her. Had she thought about it, even a few seconds ago, she would have denied all knowledge of his first words to her. It was an incredible thing, the memory.

'Nobody sent me,' she had replied. 'To be honest, I was finding it a bit overpowering in there. I'm sorry. . . I didn't mean to disturb you.'

'So you're not feeling sociable either?'

'Not in the least.'

'Good. . .we can be unsociable together.'

'Thanks for the offer,' Maggie had murmured, turning, 'but I really am not in the mood for company.'

'Neither am I, much to the the apparent incomprehension of those guys inside—which is why I suggest you join me.' He had smiled—a wearily wry smile. 'As a couple we stand a reasonable chance of being left alone—I guess they'd call it tact.'

Perhaps it had been then that the madness had taken hold of her—when he had reached to the low wall beside him and produced a magnum of champagne from which he had casually refilled the glass in his hand and offered it to her.

Without the anonymity that neither had sought to undo she would have remained Maggie Wallace, the twenty-year-old student whose spirit had just been battered almost to extinction; with it, restoration of her spirit and a million other miracles had seemed suddenly possible.

Maggie gave a dazed shake of her head as she wiped down the surface she had been working on. It had been as though her fairy godmother had waved a magic wand that promised the undoing of the savage hurt of hours before, providing a mysterious Adonis whose very touch had proved Peter's vicious claims to her frigidity a laughable lie, providing her with a lover with whom she had felt not the slightest inhibition and whose powerful appetite for passion she had been able to reciprocate with abandoned delight.

She leaned her head down till it rested against the coolness of the marble counter. What had happened in reality was that she had had too much to drink, had been picked up by an attractive, distinctly world-weary stranger and had spent the night in his bed.

The advice most commonly dished out to women who had had experiences as horrifying as the one she had had with Peter was to find someone else to undo the damage. . .but not within hours of that first horrific experience, and most certainly not with a complete stranger—a man who could have been a psychopathic killer for all she'd known about him.

All she'd known about him? She had gone out of her way to find out absolutely *nothing* about him! All she had been interested in was salving her savaged pride. And she had ended up sneaking from a stranger's bed at dawn as he had still lain sleeping, and feeling no better than trash.

'I hope you like pasta,' Slane announced on the way home, 'because that's what I'm cooking tonight—tagliatelle, bathed in a mouth-watering confection of cream, mushrooms and ham, accompanied by a fresh green salad tossed to perfection.' He took his eyes from the road for an isntant to glance at her. 'Well, I do declare the lady can still smile,' he observed drily.

'I love pasta at the best of times,' Maggie said,

forcing a light-hearted note into her words, 'and what you've just described sounds out of this world.'

Her journey through her memories had left her so thoroughly demoralised that when he had returned it had taken her all the will she possessed to try to behave normally. The speculative glances that he had flung in her direction on and off throughout the afternoon had told her that she hadn't managed to achieve what passed for normality, but mercifully he had made no comment—until his oblique remark of a few moments ago.

'Out of this world, huh?' he enquired, deadpan. 'I guess that's a pretty fair description.'

'Don't feel you have to be modest on my account,' laughed Maggie—a sound that almost made her start with surprise. 'You obviously take your cooking very seriously. Who taught you—your mother?'

'Oh, no,' he chuckled, 'most definitely not my mother. My father taught me. Now there was a guy who took his cooking very seriously.'

'Are you saying your mother can't cook?'

'No, I'm not. . .she just doesn't like it. I need to rest up before visiting my mother—she has me slaving in the kitchen day and night once I'm there. So, you see, I wasn't kidding when I said I'd marry the woman who could cook like Mrs Morrison—or my dad, for that matter.'

'If a word of what you've just said is true,' Maggie said, smiling, 'I rather like the sound of your mother. But if that's the way you feel about it why are you cooking the meal tonight?'

'Because I haven't cooked in a while and I like to keep my hand in,' he replied as they drew up in front of the house.

They took the groceries into the kitchen and put away what they wouldn't be needing for the meal; then Maggie took herself off for a shower.

All in all, facing up to the memories she had been so determined to block out hadn't done her that much harm, she told herself as she dried and got into jeans and a sweatshirt. And anyway look at Slane, she reasoned almost angrily with herself; he had behaved no differently from her that night, and she would bet her bottom dollar that he hadn't spent a second, let alone the past three years, considering himself little better than trash because of it!

'Would you mind if I watched you cooking?' Maggie asked when she returned to the kitchen.

Slane glanced up from the lettuce he had been washing, his face expressionless. 'Well, I don't know about that,' he stated with dubious caution. 'The last time I let my mother in the kitchen with me she kept me in there all night baking cookies for her—can you imagine?'

'No—not for one moment,' laughed Maggie, the unbidden thought coming to her that she liked this side of him rather a lot.

He turned from the sink, his face a picture of theatrical indignation until suddenly he smiled and Maggie felt her heart stop.

'OK, you can watch,' he conceded, transferring the lettuce to a colander, 'but you can make yourself useful drying this off while I do some chopping.'

Maggie dug in one of the cupboards for a salad spinner, convinced that her reactivating heart was about to erupt from her body. There was probably a perfectly reasonable psychological explanation for what was happening to her, she thought agitatedly—except that she was no psychologist and she felt as though she was losing her mind.

'I keep telling my mother that what she needs is a man who can cook like my father,' announced Slane as, with nonchalant expertise, he sliced the mushrooms, 'but so far she hasn't obliged.'

'You didn't really say that to her!' exclaimed Maggie, unable to keep the disquiet from her tone.

'Frequently,' he replied, before turning to her with a quizzical look. 'That shocks you?'

'I. . .well, yes—I—I suppose it does,' she stammered. 'I mean, it's not that long ago since your father died. . .'

'It's been almost three years,' he stated quietly. 'And my father sure as hell wouldn't have wanted her to go on mourning him for the rest of her life.'

'But wouldn't you mind?'

'I want the same for my mother as my father would have done—a full and happy life.' He put down the knife. 'Isn't that what you want for your mother?'

'Of course it is.'

'And has your mother remarried?'

'Yes. . .and she's very happy.'

'But I take it you're not,' he stated, returning to his work.

'You're wrong,' protested Maggie, spinning the lettuce vigorously. 'Jim, my stepfather, is one of the dearest, sweetest men I know—I love him very much.' And—better late than never—that was the truth, she thought sadly as all the old guilt came flooding back.

'So what's your problem with me suggesting that my mother should find herself someone else?'

'Slane, I'm sorry I said what I did!' she exclaimed unhappily. 'I had no right to. . . I really hadn't.'

'Old wounds, Maggie?' he asked gently, removing the salad spinner from her.

She nodded miserably. 'I feel so ashamed. I honestly meant it when I said I love Jim now.'

'But at first you hated him because you felt he was taking your father's place?'

'He and my mother married less than three years after my father died. . . Even thinking about how appallingly I behaved over it makes me feel ill.'

'And here I am, slaving over this fantastic meal,' he teased, then added gently, 'I can't say I feel too good when I think of some of the things I did right after my father died. How old were you when you lost yours?'

'Seventeen,' replied Maggie as she began laying the table. 'But I was almost nineteen when my mother started seeing Jim. . .and nothing can excuse what I put them through. My dad would have hated me for it, I know.'

'Come on, Maggie,' Slane chided, placing the salad, together with a bowl of dressing he had just mixed, on the table, 'I'm sure he would have understood—though I doubt if he'd be too pleased to see how it's still affecting you now.'

'What would you know about it?' she flared, then was immediately filled with remorse. 'I'm sorry, I really am. . . I—'

'OK, I get the message—you're sorry,' he muttered, returning to the cooker. 'The pasta's on, so if you want to see this sauce being made now's your chance.'

'I didn't mean to snap like that,' she apologised as she joined him by the cooker. 'I really am—'

'Maggie, if you apologise once more you'll not get fed,' he warned, his tone exasperated. 'Look, how about if you pour us some of that wine?' he said, motioning towards the opened bottle on the worktop beside him.

It was little wonder that she was in the state she was over him, she decided disgustedly as she got glasses and poured the wine—anything approaching a crisis in her life and she promptly went to pieces.

The meal was every bit as perfect as he had jokingly claimed it would be, and Maggie, to her complete surprise, tucked into it with the gusto it merited.

'That was wonderful,' she sighed after the last mouthful, then let out a groan.

'Yeah, that's one thing I forgot to tell you about.' He grinned. 'The food poisoning comes after.'

'I can assure you it would be worth it,' she laughed, 'but I'd just remembered I missed out on your making the sauce when I was seeing to the wine!'

'I can always give you verbal instructions any time you feel like making it. But anyway,' he added, his eyes flickering over her, 'at least the food stopped you wallowing in all that pointless angst.'

'That wasn't what I was doing!' exclaimed Maggie defensively. 'Well. . .not really,' she added half-heartedly. 'It just depresses me when I think of how disgustingly I behaved. . .'

'I know the feeling well,' he stated tonelessly. 'All this is a little too close to home for me, which is why, I guess, I gave you such a hard time of it just now. But you can't let past mistakes rule your life—that's plain crazy.'

'Yes, it is,' she said, raw bitterness spilling into her words as she realised that, while she deeply regretted the pain she had once caused her mother and Jim, it was the mistake she had made with this man who was now offering her advice that had ruled her life for the past three years.

'Yes, damn it, it is!' he exclaimed angrily. 'Hell, your mother and your stepfather have forgiven you, haven't they?'

'Completely,' replied Maggie. If he only knew how totally off the mark he was, she thought wearily.

'Just as my mother has me,' he stated, the anger still in his tone.

'Your mother?' asked Maggie bemusedly.

'I was worse than useless to my mother when my father died. OK, I stayed around and managed to keep myself together long enough to attend all the services that were held—but once that was all over, when she probably needed my support most of all, I shut myself off from her completely.'

'But of course she'd understand and forgive you,' said Maggie, even though she accepted that she was probably the last person qualified to make any statement on the subject, 'because she'd have realised that was your way of trying to cope with your grief.'

'That and my guilt,' he conceded wryly. 'You see, that's my point... Even then I knew deep down that my guilt was misplaced—but I still risked my sanity over it.'

'How long were you like that for?' asked Maggie hoarsely. As far as she knew, his father had died in a road accident. Had Slane been driving? Was that what had caused such irrational guilt in him?

He pulled a face, hunching his shoulders slightly.

'I'm sorry,' she gasped, contrition flooding her. 'I shouldn't have asked.'

'Maggie, you can ask whatever you damn well like!' he exclaimed exasperatedly. 'Whether I answer or not is up to me.'

'I'm sorry—'

'And for God's sake stop apologising!' he snapped, getting up and bringing the fruit bowl to the table. 'The last time I saw my father we had a row. . .about me and the women who were or weren't in my life,' he intoned almost wearily as he sat down. 'It should have turned into a joke, as our conversations on that subject usually did—but I guess we'd both got out of bed the wrong side that particular morning.

'He felt it was time I started looking around for a wife. . .and expressed a negative opinion or two on some of the women I'd been seeing.' He picked an orange from the bowl and contemplated it morosely. 'About an hour later the police were at the house. Some poor truck driver had had a coronary at the wheel—my dad and the occupant of another car the truck had hit had been killed instantly.'

Maggie heard her own sharp intake of breath, but was incapable of uttering a word.

'I guess it was the shock and the grief that made it impossible for me to reason coherently,' he continued in that same, starkly blank tone, 'but the only constant thing in my mind was that our last words had been exchanged in anger.

'I must have had a shred of reason left in me, though, because I didn't take off right away—I fought with myself every day just to stay put with my mother and family. But the need to get away just got worse. . .

'Then one day I came across an invitation I'd received to the wedding of a guy I'd known at Yale and who was now doing research in England. I didn't even remember him that well and hadn't planned on going, but he was getting married in England to a girl from Sussex and, wretched though it was, that was as good an excuse as any I could come up with for putting as much distance as I could between me and my family.'

Maggie's blood had frozen in her veins; there was no need for her to ask when this had happened—the date was already engraved in her mind.

'Who knows? Maybe I went there with some crazy idea of finding me the wife that would have pleased my father,' Slane muttered, with a bitter laugh. 'But naturally things didn't work out quite like that,' he added dismissively, returning the orange to the bowl, 'and I was back in the States inside three days—stunned back into relative normality.'

Maggie's heart was hammering so madly and her mouth was so dry that she wasn't sure she could cope with speech—but she forced the words from herself anyway. 'How do you mean—stunned?'

'The details aren't that important,' he drawled, rising. 'It's putting them behind you that matters. Coffee?'

'No, thanks, I'll stick with this,' she muttered, her hand shaking as she touched her wine glass. No wonder he hadn't recognised her, she thought with a sharp stab of mortification; she was merely a detail—and plainly a most unpleasant one—that he had put behind him!

'I've been meaning to ask you,' she said, making a concerted effort to distract herself from her wounding thoughts. 'Have you been able to tell anything from the tests so far?'

He returned to the table with a pot of coffee, his expression wry. 'No, but I wouldn't expect to,' he said, then glanced across at her, something that she couldn't quite put her finger on in his expression. 'Our test results wil have to be put on computer for cross-cellular comparisons with the original plant—only then will we know.'

He poured himself some coffee, then looked across at her with an expression close to irritation on his face. 'Just what did Connor say to you about all this the night I arrived?' he demanded suddenly.

Maggie returned his look with one of genuine puzzlement.

'I know him too well. He'll have got it into his head that I'm here to chase a rainbow for my father, and he'll be fretting about how I'll take it if I don't succeed.'

'Perhaps that's because he knows *you* too well,' she said quietly. 'Your involving yourself to the extent you have with the tests must have told him something.'

'It's obvious I'm doing them because of my father!' he exclaimed impatiently. 'He thrived on this sort of interaction with Maurice... Hell, it's probably more because of poor old Maurice that I've gotten myself this personally involved,' he sighed. 'He must have had pretty mixed emotions, continuing with the test growths. Dad's death came as a terrible blow to him—'

He broke off with a shake of his head. 'I'd arranged for someone else to come here, but when it came to it I knew I owed it to them both to come myself.'

'And, from what you've said of Maurice, if he's had no luck this time you'll keep coming back,' murmured Maggie, feeling peculiarly close to tears.

'Did no one ever tell you there are certain thoughts best left unsaid for fear they'll come true?' Slane groaned through his laughter. 'Though if this darned plant could be produced and actually do what it's claimed to be able to do—now that really would be something.'

'I know there's no putting back the clock,' she said

wistfully, 'but I can't help wondering whether a drug like that might have saved my father's life.'

'Your father's death was allergy-related?'

She nodded, pain searing through her. 'It all happened so quickly; my mother and I could hardly take it in. My dad had been away on a trip to Burundi and Uganda with a group from the school at which he taught. The trip was a nationwide prize the pupils had won. The only reason my dad went was because one of the other teachers had to drop out at the last minute.

'Two or three of the group, including my father, picked up a bug while they were out there. Diagnosing it was pretty straightforward, and so was the treatment. . .except that my dad had a violently adverse reaction to the drugs used to treat it—'

'You poor kid,' he muttered as she broke off with a helpless shrug, reaching over and taking one of her hands in his briefly.

'At first I was so devastated at having lost him that it didn't even occur to me to consider how much worse it could have been. . .for my dad, that is. He was so much his normal self when they admitted him into the hospital—joking about him being the odd one out and the others popping their pills and reacting as they were supposed to. There was no reason for him to be worried, and he wasn't.

'His last words to me were to remind my mother to get the car serviced—we'd planned a trip to the Lake District that weekend. That night he drifted into a coma in his sleep. He never came out of it.'

For several seconds Slane sat there motionless, his eyes on her but their far-away look denying any sight of her. Then he gave a start, as though emerging from deep thought.

'And now you plan to follow your father into teach-ing,' he stated, his tone verging on abrupt.

'I'll be twenty-four soon—it's about time I sorted out a proper career for myself,' she replied, wondering at the sudden change in him. He didn't strike her as the type of person who would open up often, not even to those closest to him, and now he was probably regret-ting what little he had revealed to her.

'And, of course, there's the fact that Connor's sold Body and Soul,' he murmured. 'I guess that helped influence your career decision.'

'Minimally,' replied Maggie, telling herself that she was being grossly over-sensitive in her interpretation of his tone. 'But whether Connor had kept it or not I'd already decided it was time to move on.'

He made no comment as he lifted the wine bottle and topped up their glasses. Then he picked up his own glass and touched it to hers.

'To your new career,' he said, 'and to the success of Maurice's wonder plant.'

Maggie raised her glass to her lips.

'And, of course,' he added, a sardonic smile skim-ming his lips, 'to the billions of dollars to be raked in from such a success.'

Maggie lowered her glass, her expression dumbfounded.

'Why so shocked, Maggie?' he drawled. 'Surely it must have occurred to you we'd be talking megabucks if this thing ever lived up to Maurice's claims for it?'

'I. . . N-no, it hadn't occurred to me,' she stammered, unable to comprehend the bitterness of the disappoint-ment she was experiencing.

'But the idea obviously offends your sensibilities in some way,' he observed silkily.

'There's no reason why it should,' she replied, her every instinct warning her that he was playing some sort of convoluted game with her—but what or why she had no idea. 'After all, you're a businessman. . .'

'And what else do businessmen do but make money whenever and wherever an opportunity presents itself? Is that what you're saying, Maggie?'

'I wasn't actually saying anything in particular!' she exclaimed, leaping to her feet and beginning to clear the table.

'You don't *actually* ever say anything much in particular, do you, Maggie?' he drawled, rising also.

'How dare you?' she gasped, slamming the dish in her hands down onto the table in the heat of the fury possessing her. 'I've just been telling you what happened to my father and you have the gall to turn round and—'

'Damn it, that's just what I mean!' he exclaimed harshly. 'What happened to your father was an appalling tragedy, as was what happened to mine. . . But for a brief moment, when you were speaking about him and about your mother, you came over as *real*—not the cardboard cut-out you—'

'You're sick—do you know that?' howled Maggie, beside herself with fury. 'Just because you regret letting your macho front slip and showing you have some feelings, don't you dare try to take it out on me!'

'OK, so my timing was lousy and I apologise,' he stated grudgingly. 'But you're the one putting up the front, Maggie, and every now and then it slips. And, believe me, I intend finding out what it is you're hiding behind that Miss Prim exterior!'

'You really do talk some rubbish!' she exclaimed scathingly, while a cacophany of alarms bells clanged inside her. 'Which is probably why I have such difficulty communicating with you.'

'But there's one way we seem to have no problem communicating with one another,' he stated icily, the insolent sweep of his eyes over her leaving her in no doubt as to the exact meaning behind his words. 'Perhaps we'll just have to resort to that if all else fails.'

CHAPTER FIVE

'MAGGIE, I want to apologise for my behaviour last night,' said Slane, looking drawn and bleary-eyed as he entered the kitchen. 'I can't blame you for walking out on me the way you did, but you missed out on the apology I should have given you right then.'

'The subject we'd been discussing was hardly one to make either of us feel at his or her best,' said Maggie, puzzled, more than a mite gratified to see that he looked almost as bad as she felt, but wishing that her hands would stop shaking as she poured him coffee. 'Apology accepted,' she said, her eyes managing to avoid his as she handed him the cup. 'And now, let's forget about it. Would you like me to scramble you some eggs?'

'No, thanks—coffee's fine for me,' he muttered, still standing. 'And as for last night. . . I was apologising for the way I said what I did but not for saying it. So no, I don't want to forget about it.'

Maggie felt her head swim. And little wonder, she thought wearily; it had been churning chaotically for the best part of the night, composing ludicrous speeches, half of which began with 'I know you remember me, Slane. . .' and the other half with 'You don't remember me, Slane, but. . .'

'What am I supposed to say?' she exclaimed exasperatedly. 'I'm the way I am, and if you see me as a cardboard cut-out of a real person there's nothing I can do about it.'

'You do yourself an injustice,' he drawled, his look icy.

'Something *you* wouldn't dream of,' she retorted acidly. What a perfect start to the day! she thought.

'Are you ready?' he demanded, downing his coffee in one gulp.

'Yes,' she answered. As ready as I'll ever be, she fumed to herself as she marched past him and out into the hall.

'I guess one of the things that puzzles me, and, believe me, there are a few,' he continued relentlessly once they were on their way, 'is how a woman of your obvious talents has taken so much time deciding on how she's to put those talents to work.'

'I haven't exactly been bumming around doing nothing,' replied Maggie, having to exert considerable control over herself not to betray the anger she felt at those arrogantly drawled words. 'Not that it's any of your business,' she added as an afterthought in deference to her anger.

'I agree, it isn't,' he murmured, managing to sound like reason personified. 'I guess you could put it down to a mixture of curiosity and envy on my part,' he added, with a sigh.

'Envy?' enquired Maggie, suspicion joining her anger.

'What guy wouldn't be envious?' he asked in that same innocently reasonable tone. 'To have a girl Friday at his beck and call, who's not only brainy but also very beautiful. . . I'd say my cousin Connor's a very lucky—'

'I beg your pardon?' she gasped, her mind balking wildly at what she prayed was the misinterpretation it had given to his words. 'I think you'd better explain what you've just said.'

'Well, the brains and the beauty don't need any explaining,' he murmured, 'so I guess it must be the girl Friday. Perhaps I've got it wrong, but that's the way I see you in relation to Connor.

'When he's left with Body and Soul on his hands, Maggie's there to step in. The two of you are cosy enough for him not to think twice about leaving you installed in his place, even though his housekeeper's on vacation. And when he doesn't want to leave me high and dry who is it who steps in and makes everything OK?'

'All right, the guilty secret's out—and what chance had it against a mind as shrewd as yours?' exclaimed Maggie with theatrical abandon, suddenly not knowing whether to laugh or cry. 'Connor and I have been having this mad, passionate affair for. . .oh, goodness knows how long!'

'So—are the pair of you planning on marrying, or is that another of those things that aren't any of my business?'

Maggie glanced across at him in alarm—surely he couldn't be serious? But his expression was giving away nothing as he negotiated the car out of the traffic and speeded towards the coast road.

'I see,' he murmured after a while. 'It's none of my business.'

'For heaven's sake stop being so ridiculous!' snapped Maggie. 'Why on earth are you behaving like this?'

'Come on now, Maggie; don't tell me you've never heard of wealthy older men being hooked by beautiful women less than half their age?'

'You. . . My God, I don't believe I'm. . .' Her gibbered words spluttered to a halt when the sound of his laughter finally penetrated her fury. 'You really are unspeakable!'

'Yeah,' he choked, 'but at least I got a reaction.'

'You'd make an insinuation like that simply to get a reaction?' she gasped.

'And I sure as hell succeeded.'

'So why is the idea so overwhelmingly hilarious?' she demanded, his continued laughter rekindling her fury and fuelling it with indignation. 'After all, as you've just pointed out, lots of older men marry younger women.'

'Yes. . .but Connor?' He had barely got the words out before he was convulsed by yet another infuriating bout of laughter. He was still chuckling to himself as they turned down the lane approaching the estate. 'Our luck's in — the gates are open.'

'Why shouldn't a younger woman want to marry the Prof?' demanded Maggie, her indignation finding a new champion.

'I'm sure there are quite a number of nubile young things who'd be only too happy to snap him up,' replied Slane, 'but there's no way a guy like Connor is ever going to make their dreams come true.' He pulled the car up in front of the laboratory. 'How on earth did we get into a conversation as crazy as this?' he asked as he got out of the car.

'We got into it because you introduced it,' accused Maggie as she followed him into the lab.

'Yeah — so I did,' he drawled, stripping off his outer clothing. 'To get a reaction from you.' He grinned suddenly. 'Though I didn't get quite the reaction I'd expected.'

She ought to drop this ridiculous conversation here

and now, Maggie told herself as she changed. She followed him into the lab.

'So what sort of reaction did you expect?' she asked with a perversity that made her wonder about herself.

'Either that you'd get mad and yell,' he murmured complacently, 'or that you'd give me the Miss Prim routine.'

She watched him in silence as he prepared and divided up the plants that John had left, wondering why she wasn't gibbering with rage. He glanced up, catching her unawares, and blew her a noisy kiss. Her eyes widened in shock; then she turned on her heel and walked back into the ante-room.

Her heart was hammering like a piston gone berserk as she opened up the tiny kitchenette and prepared the coffee.

'Maggie, is it any wonder you have me thoroughly confused?' he muttered from behind her, his hands descending on her shoulders before she could turn to escape. 'When I try to rile you you laugh it off. Then the next moment you're stomping off because I jokingly throw you a kiss.'

'I didn't stomp off,' she ground out from between clenched teeth. 'I merely came out here to make coffee.' Only his hands were touching her, but her body was tensed in an almost painful longing to be drawn back and pressed against the length of his.

'Maggie, I want to take you in my arms,' he whispered against her hair. 'Don't worry—I shan't. But I'd like to ask you to indulge me by trying something.'

His soft words made her feel giddy, reminded her of that single night when he had been the stranger whose every passionate demand she had fearlessly indulged, as he had hers.

'Blank your mind and pretend I've just arrived now, instead of the other evening—can you do that?'

She nodded, conscious of every nerve in her willing him to change his mind and take her in his arms.

'But can you also blank your mind of all the negative baggage it's carrying concerning me and just talk to me the way you would a regular guy?'

She nodded again, her nails digging into her palms with the effort it was taking to still the unbearable awareness trembling through her.

He released her and was back in the lab by the time she had gathered herself sufficiently to turn to face him. She made the coffee, refusing to indulge her mind in its tortuous 'Does this mean he can't possibly remember—or am I deluding myself?' routine. To hell with it, she thought recklessly; she was out of her mind anyway, so if he wanted to play games she'd play them!

'Excuse me, Mr Fitzpatrick,' she called, 'but how do you take your coffee?'

'Cut it out, Maggie,' he called back, amused exasperation in his tone, 'or I'll think you're not taking this seriously.'

Composing her face, she entered the lab with two mugs. 'White with no sugar?' she murmured, handing him her own drink.

'Gee, thanks, Maggie,' he replied, and took a swig. 'Perfect,' he murmured, with a smug grin, and chuckled outright when she hastily swapped the mugs. 'And don't even *think* of suggesting I take you through the dissection routine,' he warned.

'The way the rules seem to be changing all the time I'm sure I'm going to get terribly confused,' sighed Maggie meekly, hamming it to the hilt in her efforts to drag her mind from its preoccupation with the way she had felt in the ante-room. 'So, tell me, Mr Fitzpatrick, do you do this sort of thing for a living?' she asked as she set up her first slide.

'Maggie!'

She made a show of racking her brains. 'How old are you?' she asked eventually.

He flashed her a disapproving look. 'Thirty-two. How old are you?'

'Twenty-three—nearly twenty-four. Are you mar–ried?'

'No. But tell me, Maggie, are you always this personal with guys you've just met?'

For an instant she froze, then decided, To hell with it. Perhaps his words were loaded, perhaps they weren't—but from now on she refused to take them at anything other than their face value.

'Always—it's one of my faults.'

'Good, it's one of mine too, so we should get on just fine,' he murmured, marking a slide. 'I know you were one of Connor's students,' he launched in, barely pausing to take a breath, 'but how come you've remained on such close terms with him since then?'

Maggie looked across at him, frowning.

'He is family, after all,' he murmured, as though answering her unspoken accusation. 'And I'm curious, anyway.'

True enough, conceded Maggie, and, anyway, there was no reason not to explain what—now that she came to think of it—might have struck him as a rather unusual friendship, even though Connor still remained in close touch with dozens of his ex-students.

'I had a bit of a personal crisis a few months before I sat my finals.' A crisis in which you featured rather heavily, she added in silent cynicism. 'I thought I was

managing to hide it brilliantly until the Prof took me to
one side and asked me what was wrong.'

'I'm surprised he didn't tip you over the edge,'
muttered Slane prosaically. 'We Fitzpatricks aren't
normally renowned for our tact and understanding.'

Maggie gave an involuntary smile. 'That thought has
occurred to me once or twice since I've really got to
know him,' she said. 'But I've a feeling he was pretty
vulnerable himself just then. . . It wasn't that long after
your father had died. I suppose, in a way, I was in
desperate need of a father figure—even though I was
getting on well with my stepfather by then—and
Connor, I'm sure much to his surprise, stepped into the
role.

'I'm not saying he counselled me or anything as
tangible as that—in fact, he set me so much extra work
I hardly had time to wallow. . .and—' She broke off
with a diffident shrug.

'And what, Maggie?'

'It's just that when I'm feeling low I tend to think
about my father a lot. I talked to Connor about him.
Later, when his wife died. . . I went to him, knowing he
knew I'd understand his need just to be able to talk
about her.'

'That's something an awful lot of people just don't
seem to understand,' sighed Slane. 'It nearly drove me
crazy the way people would talk about anything and
anyone but my dad after his death, as though they were
afraid that mentioning him would somehow upset those
of us who loved him.' For a while he continued working
in silence. 'So how did he talk you into working for
Body and Soul?' he asked eventually.

'I think you know Connor better than that,' said
Maggie quietly. 'It took me a long time to realise that

he would never have suggested it if he hadn't felt I needed that sort of environment then, probably more than the shop needed me... I was still in a bit of an emotional mess.'

'And how long is it since you stopped needing it?' he asked, his tone not in the least contentious.

'Let's put it this way—' she smiled '—the Prof's been dropping heavy hints about my moving on for almost a year now.'

'So he's sold the place from under you?' chuckled Slane.

'Oh, no—he's been looking for a buyer whom Marjorie would have approved of since a few months after her death—someone who would keep the old staff on and develop the business along the lines she would have wanted.'

They chatted with comparative ease, sometimes teasing, sometimes serious, lapsing into prolonged silences when the work demanded it, then breaking back into conversation when it didn't. On and off, Slane spoke of Marjorie, then later of his stays in Dublin with Marjorie and Connor, his deep affection for them both colouring his words.

'They used to call my mom and dad the Yankee lovebirds—whereas Mom and Dad always called them the Irish lovebirds,' he chuckled. 'And what about your love life, Maggie?'

'Pretty average,' she muttered, completely thrown by the sheer unexpectedness of the question. Average? She hadn't let a man within an arm's length of her since...since him!

'What's average to some might be considered hectic by others,' he observed drily. 'So—when were you last in love?'

'That's not fair,' she protested, a million alarm bells sounding off in her. 'No one would ask a person they'd just met a question like that!'

'Except us, Maggie,' he murmured, raising his head from what he was examining and batting his eyelids unashamedly at her. 'The fault we have in common— remember?' He returned his eyes to his work, then murmured, 'So when was it?'

'It was so long ago I can hardly remember,' she responded flippantly.

'Maggie, you're only twenty-three, for God's sake!' he exclaimed with undisguised scepticism. 'Just how far back can you go?'

'Slane, have you noticed how the alkaloids in this particular batch—?'

'What I've really noticed is how you're ducking the question,' he interrupted smoothly. 'Does that mean you've never been in love?'

'Of course I have!' she exclaimed defensively, and immediately wondered why she had reacted that way— after all, it was hardly a crime never to have been in love.

'There's no law that says you have to have been,' murmured Slane, his words disconcertingly mirroring her own belated thoughts.

'I know there isn't, but I have been—in love, that is—once.'

'We might as well get this lot entered up,' he muttered, straightening. 'Are you through with that yet?'

'Just give me a few seconds,' she said, barely able to contain the relief flooding her as he moved to the counter at right angles to where they were working.

'Only the once?' came his drawling, persistent enquiry.

'Slane, let me finish this, will you?' she groaned, hunching her shoulders as though utterly engrossed.

Even had her relationship with Peter not ended as horrifically as it did, it would have ended sooner or later—with her inevitable realisation that she wasn't and never really had been in love with him... The closest she had ever come to experiencing what she felt love should be had been in the arms of a complete stranger.

'Right—here you are,' she said, her tone calm, almost detached. 'Would you like me to write some of them up for you?'

'No, that's OK, but I wouldn't say no to a coffee... Hell, what time is it anyway?' he exclaimed, glancing down at his watch. 'I thought you were supposed to be reminding us about lunch—now it's way too late!'

'I'm afraid that was part of the baggage that you recommended I discard,' murmured Maggie as she took herself off to make the coffee.

The truth was that she had completely lost track of the time, she thought edgily, her head beginning to swim from the hornets' nest of thoughts buzzing inside it.

Despite the nagging legacy of what bordered on shame, left her by that one night with Slane, there were certain facts about it which she had never attempted to deny. She had come to him not simply in ignorance of the pleasures of lovemaking, but bruised and damaged by her one brutal experience of it.

She gave a small shudder at the very thought of the appalling irresponsibility of the risk she had taken... But for all her inexperience she had tasted perfection in his arms and had recognised it as such.

'Are you still in love with this guy, Maggie?' he asked when she returned with their drinks.

'When am I going to get a chance to ask you some questions?' she demanded, marvelling at the laughing indignation she had managed to inject into her words, while her heart sank at his terrier-like return to the subject.

'Ask away.' He grinned, taking a gulp from his cup.

'I. . . How many times have you been in love?' She began seriously questioning her own sanity the instant the words popped out.

'I guess it must be the way I was reared, but I've never regarded love as something to be fallen in and out of,' he said almost guardedly. 'My father and Connor both had pretty wild reputations before they found my mother and Marjorie, but once they fell in love—corny though it may sound—that's the way they stayed.'

He put his cup down, his expression pensive. 'Though how things would have been had my mother and Marjorie not remained every bit as in love as they did is a whole different ball game. I guess the most dangerous part of falling in love is finding the right person to do it with.'

'So I take it the answer to my question is that you've never been in love,' said Maggie, injecting a flippancy into her words that she was far from feeling. . . In fact, she was having great difficulty in working out exactly what it was she was feeling, except that down would have been a decided improvement on whatever it was.

He gave a slight shrug. 'OK, so my views on the subject are—what? Simplistic? Over-idealistic?' he muttered, returning to the ledger he had been writing in. 'Or just plain unattainable in this day and age? I can't say I haven't been infatuated a number of times and once I even—' He broke off with a harsh laugh. 'But you're right—I've never been in love.'

'What makes you think your views are any different from those most people start out with?' asked Maggie, an edge of bitterness creeping into her tone.

'Experience,' he retorted brusquely, and carried on writing. 'And what effect has experience had on the views you started out with, Maggie?'

What indeed? she wondered bitterly. 'I haven't really thought about it,' she replied, and made a show of concentrating on her work.

'Yeah—and pigs fly.'

'I'm sure they do if you say so!' she exclaimed angrily, feeling inexplicably close to breaking-point. 'And now I'm afraid I'm going to be a terrible spoil-sport and opt out of this little game of yours—not that I'd ever have joined in if I'd realised that all it would entail was me being grilled like this by you.'

'How many times do you need telling?' he laughed. 'You can ask all the questions you like. . .so you can stop snapping at me like—'

'I'm not snapping,' she interrupted furiously, then astounded them both by bursting into tears.

'Maggie, I was only teasing!' he exclaimed, rushing to her side and swinging round the high stool on which she sat till she was facing him. 'Maggie, what's gotten into you?' he asked anxiously, reaching a hand towards her and having it batted angrily aside. 'Whatever I've said that's upset you like this, I'm sorry,' he muttered, lifting her from the chair and holding her gently against him.

'I'm *not* upset!' she protested futilely. 'Oh, God. . . I feel such a fool!'

'No—it seems I've been the fool,' he sighed against her hair.

'No. . .you don't understand,' she protested incoherently. Not that she did either—she was behaving in a manner that was completely alien to her and, worse, hadn't the slightest idea why. And she wasn't likely to find out if he didn't let go of her, she thought distractedly as his arms shifted slightly around her and a sensuous heat spread through her like wildfire.

'I mean. . .it's not you,' she choked, the feelings which were heightening within her almost suffocating her. 'It's. . . There are things I don't want to remember.'

'But if you don't lay your ghost to rest they'll haunt you for ever,' he whispered huskily, his arms moving then tightening swiftly around her. 'Maggie, I— No!' he groaned as a palpable heat surged between them, and he released her abruptly. 'I'm sorry,' he muttered. 'I didn't mean for that to happen.'

He glanced down at his watch and spoke with his eyes still on it. 'Look, let's just call it a day here,' he suggested unsteadily. 'You go fix yourself up and I'll clear away in here.'

Grateful that her legs had actually managed the brief journey, Maggie closed the door of the tiny cloakroom behind her and gazed at her tear-streaked reflection with eyes wide with apprehension. Just what exactly was happening to her?

Despite what her experience with Slane had revealed to her about her own capacity for passion, she had kept men at a strict distance ever since that night. It hadn't been a conscious decision on her part, but it was one, she had found, to her consternation, that tended to heighten most men's interest rather than putting them off. Any lingering shame she might have felt for what had happened with Slane was immaterial—the blame had always been Peter's... But had it?

'Maggie, are you OK?'

'I'm coming!' She splashed cold water on her face and patted it dry, then untied her hair and ran her fingers through it.

'Maggie, I really am sorry. I—'

'Now I know how you felt when I kept apologising last night,' she said, the intended jocularity of her words failing to materialise.

She took the coat he held out to her, her eyes unable to meet his as she did so. He hadn't liked what had flared between them just then, not one little bit, she thought numbly, and now he couldn't get away from this enclosed space fast enough.

'I thought we'd eat out tonight,' he said as he held the outer door open for her. 'Is that OK with you?'

'Yes, that's fine,' she said. The house—another relatively enclosed space, she thought wryly before deciding that she was being paranoiac.

'I'll not irritate you by repeating how sorry I am that I upset you, but I meant what I said about laying your ghosts,' he said once they were on their way. 'But, there again, I guess I'm just being nosy... I want to know what makes you tick, but you've already worked that out for yourself, haven't you, Maggie?'

The trouble was, she thought wearily, that there was nothing she had been able to work out about him.

'If you think hearing about my non-existent love life has any bearing on what makes me tick, then I'm afraid you're in for a big disappointment,' she retorted, then added exasperatedly, 'Look, let's just say I came to grief at what you described as the most dangerous part of falling in love—I chose the wrong person.'

Except that that wasn't quite the truth, she thought dazedly. She had done it all back to front—chosen the right person at the wrong time and, because her eyes had been glued shut, hadn't even known it.

'And you're still in love with him,' he said, his words a statement rather than a question.

She glanced over at the shadowy outline of his profile and felt her heart lurch painfully. The only explanation for what was going on in her head, she reasoned in complete panic, was a mental breakdown!

'How long ago did you make this mistake?' he asked quietly. 'OK, OK,' he soothed in alarm as Maggie responded with a soft choking sound.

He reached over and briefly patted the hands clenched in her lap. 'As I've already admitted, we Fitzpatricks aren't exactly renowned for our tact, but—' He broke off with a huge sigh. 'But nothing—it's time this one had a go at keeping his big mouth shut.'

CHAPTER SIX

ONCE again Maggie was conscious of eyes following them as they were led to their table in the restaurant that Slane had claimed served the best fish to be had anywhere.

At least this time she wasn't looking like a drowned rat, she thought, thankful that she had put her hair up and had worn the silk shirtwaister that her mother and Jim had brought her back from a trip to Italy, because its deep blue exactly matched her eyes.

She had been in two minds whether or not to bring the dress, she remembered, and gave silent thanks that she had as she became uncomfortably aware of the stratospheric level of smartness and sophistication of those around her.

'I'd no idea how trendy this place had become,' muttered Slane, plainly none too impressed by this fact. 'I hope I don't have to take back what I said about the food,' he added morosely, opening his menu and studying it.'

Maggie, who had caught sight of one or two vaguely familiar faces at the tables near theirs, opened hers too and buried her nose in it. She wasn't given to gawping at celebrities, but she was half tempted to do so now just to annoy him.

It wasn't as though she had expected him to do cartwheels of joy just because she had taken a bit of trouble with her appearance, but neither had she expected the blank wall she had met—and he had barely spoken a word during the taxi ride here.

She gave a small start, realising that she was developing a tendency to become bogged down in the morass of her own thoughts. She forced herself to look at the menu before her and immediately found herself wondering whether she would be capable of eating anything at all.

'How about some oysters to start with?' asked Slane, closing his menu.

Maggie hesitated, then shook her head. 'I don't think I'll have anything to start with, thanks.'

He leaned back in his chair once he had given their orders, his eyes coolly speculative. 'You seem very pensive,' he murmured, his tone as cool as his eyes.

'Do I?' she enquired stiffly.

'You do,' he said. 'Those really must be some memories I've stirred up in you.'

And all of them extremely unpleasant, thought Maggie wearily, an involuntary smile of relief darting to her face as a waiter arrived with the oysters.

'I'll trade you an oyster for another smile,' murmured Slane, then broke off to taste the wine a second waiter had arrived with. 'Have some, Maggie,' he urged when the waiter moved the bottle to her glass. 'This is a wine not be passed up.'

Maggie nodded to the waiter, Slane's remark about trading for a smile ricocheting disruptively around her head. To distract herself from its effect she took a sip of the wine and found it deliciously fresh and light on her palate.

'Good?'

'Very,' she replied.

'How about one of these to go with it?' he said,

loosening an oyster from its shell, squeezing some lemon on it, then offering it to her across the table. 'What's wrong?' he enquired as she hesitated. 'Afraid of the effect it might have on you?'

'I've never eaten an oyster before,' she admitted, racking her brains in an effort to remember what effect they were supposed to have.

'OK.' He grinned. 'Just open your mouth and, when I tip it in, swallow.'

She did as he instructed, unable to suppress a shudder of disgust as she swallowed.

'Not impressed?' he chuckled, then downed two in a row himself as Maggie dived for her wine glass and took a hearty gulp from it.

'It was like taking in a mouthful of sea water!' she exclaimed, watching in disbelief as he downed several more. 'How on earth could anyone think something like that could possibly act as an aphrodisiac?' she added incredulously as her brain belatedly responded to its earlier racking.

'They say the more unpalatable you find them, the greater their effect in that respect,' he murmured, topping up both their glasses.

'You're joking!' exclaimed Maggie, and immediately began subjecting her brain to another bout of racking.

'Of course I am,' he chuckled. 'Though I sure had you worried for a moment there.'

'Of course you didn't,' she laughed. 'The whole thing's nonsense anyway.'

'Let's hope so,' he murmured, his eyes teasing as he raised the last of the oysters to his lips, 'otherwise you're going to have your hands full with me tonight—' He broke off, his eyes widening theatrically. 'I think I could have phrased that a mite better,' he added, then

turned and gave his attention to the waiters who had
arrived and were boning their orders of sole on a side-
trolley.

Oh, God, she almost groaned aloud as something
clicked almost painfully into place inside her. She had
been letting the fact of the past get in the way and
confuse her. But the past had nothing to do with the
here and now.

The man before her undeniably had his negative
side, but, all in all, he was attractive, witty, sophisti-
cated and at times immensely likable. Had she in fact
only met him a few days ago, and had no past to
confuse her, she wouldn't have had the slightest difficulty in accepting that she had fallen in love with him.

'Perfection,' he murmured after taking his first
mouthful of sole. 'Talking of which, you're looking
pretty perfect yourself, Maggie. That colour suits you;
what is it—midnight-blue?'

Maggie nodded, the unexpectedness of his question
throwing her almost as much as the thoughts it had just
displaced. 'Yes, I suppose it is,' she muttered vaguely.
'Why do you ask?'

'Because it's the same colour as your eyes,' he
replied, with a smile that turned everything in her
upside down. 'Why are you looking at me like that,
Maggie?'

'Like what?' she croaked, terrified that this crazy
infatuation, or whatever it was she felt for him, might
be written all over her.

'As though you don't believe me.' He flashed her a
smile and continued eating. 'Just as you didn't believe
me when I expressed an opinion that you were
beautiful.'

Maggie forced herself to eat. The fish was fresh and

moist and exquisitely cooked, yet she was so tensed up that she feared she would choke on it. One thing was certain, she thought distractedly; she couldn't cope with much more of this. . . Before this evening was over she was going to have to bring up the past, if only for her sanity's sake.

'Midnight-blue eyes—how could I ever forget them?' he sighed, casually spearing a sautéed potato from the plate that she had just abandoned. Then his eyes caught hers across the table, impaling them on icicles.

'We're back to the subject you seem hell-bent on not facing, Maggie,' he said with chilling softness. 'You can bury all the ghosts you like, but not me—and why not? Because you have the misfortune to be one of the few ghosts I have. . .or perhaps a better description is that you're the only real skeleton I have in my closet. . . And I intend rattling you out of it.'

This time there was no 'does he?' or 'doesn't he?' for her to contend with, even though for one moment of complete panic her mind still clung to them. When she attempted to speak no sound emerged.

'Slane Fitzpatrick! Tell me I'm not seeing things! My God, it really is you!'

Her mouth still dry with shock, Maggie watched as a tall, vivacious woman with a startling crop of red curls whisked a seat from the next table. By the time the woman had drawn it up .to their table Maggie was observing her with feelings of detachment bordering on complete absence.

'Gee, I realised this was the in place around these parts,' the woman breezed on in strong American accents, 'but not that it attracted big shots like Slane Fitzpatrick. What did you do, Slane—jet in for the evening?'

'Go away, Hattie,' drawled Slane, his jaw tightening ominously.

'"Go away", he says!' chortled the woman while at the same time casting an appraising eye over Maggie, who gazed back at her blankly. 'The last time I saw this guy—'

'Hattie,' growled Slane, though there was a discernible trace of amusement in his exasperation.

'Come on, Slane, you're perfectly safe,' she wheedled, winking at the still expressionless Maggie. 'I'm a reformed character—I've moved up-market from the gossip sheets. I'm over here doing a piece for a magazine on this great new Irish group—' She broke off, pulling a face as she glanced across the room.

'The trouble is I was supposed to be interviewing the lead singer alone over a meal this evening and the darned guy's brought his girlfriend along. It's a wonder the management hasn't complained about them bringing their own food!' she exclaimed, rolling her eyes. 'They've spent the last hour all but eating one another.'

'Maggie and I were about to have a nibble on one another, too, until you so rudely interrupted us,' murmured Slane drily, shaking his head as a waiter arrived and proffered the menu. 'I'll just have coffee. How about you, Maggie?'

'Just coffee, thanks,' she replied, having considerable difficulty in applying her mind to the present.

'Make that coffee for three,' murmured Hattie, giving the waiter a dazzling smile.

'The third one to be served at the lady's own table,' drawled Slane.

'He's only kidding,' laughed the American woman, who then turned her attention to Maggie. 'I guess we'll

wait all night for Slane to get around to introducing us.
I'm Hattie Lang,' she said, stretching out a hand.

Maggie robotically returned the handshake, remembering to order a smile to her lips as she did so.

'It must make quite a change for you, Hattie,'
murmured Slane, watching the exchange through narrowed eyes, 'not having someone draw back in horror
at the sound of your name. In case you're interested,
Maggie, Hattie feeds a string of the most scurrilous
gossip columns—'

'How many times do I have to tell you?' exclaimed
the journalist indignantly. 'I've left all that behind. . .
which is just as well,' she added archly, flashing Maggie
a teasing grin, 'because if I hadn't a certain movie
actress we all adore would be reading what the love of
her life is getting up to while she's not around. Tell me,
Slane, does Felicity Field actually know you're in
Ireland?'

Slane's reply was lost on Maggie, whose mind had
been reactivated by images of the willowy, Titian-
haired actress, renowned for the astuteness of her mind
as well as for her exceptional beauty. Then she thought
of the amount of time she had spent striving to look
her best this evening, and almost laughed aloud.

'So tell me, Maggie,' murmured Hattie, 'what's your
role in this heartbreaker's life? Or are you—?'

'Drop it, Hattie!' snapped Slane, flashing Maggie a
warning look.

'Talk about giving a dog a bad name,' groaned Hattie
as the coffee arrived, 'though I guess in a way I deserve
it,' she sighed, smiling ruefully at Maggie.

'He's a very difficult guy to pin down—whether
you're a journalist or a gal who's fallen for him. . . Hell,
I'm sounding like a real bitch,' she muttered, picking

up her coffee-cup and taking a drink from it. 'Those two I'm with were so busy chomping on one another I ended up consoling myself with the wine bottle... Look, I'm sorry—I really am.'

'Poor Hattie,' chuckled Slane. 'I guess it looks as though we'll have to offer you a ride back into town.'

'Darn it, I'd just called for a cab when I spotted you,' groaned Hattie. 'It should be here in a couple of minutes.'

She turned to Maggie. 'Don't you pay any attention to what I've been saying about this guy.' She smiled, then dropped her voice to a stage whisper. 'And don't you let him know I've said it, but of all the hotshots I've tailed in my time this one's special... He may play around with the good-time gals, but it won't be one of them who catches him.'

'Just how much wine *did* you console yourself with, Hattie?' drawled Slane irritably.

'Not enough to forget what a lot of folks might not suspect of you,' she replied, nodding as a waiter signalled that her taxi had arrived. 'That you have this streak of old-fashioned—' She broke off as she rose to her feet, frowning as though mentally searching for something. 'I guess the only word for it is morality—yes, you've a streak of morality running through you, Slane.'

She turned to Maggie. 'It was good meeting you, Maggie, even though you plainly didn't feel it safe to say a word to me,' she teased. 'I'm back off to the States tomorrow,' she announced to Slane, reaching over and ruffling his hair. 'Whether or not you were about to start chomping on Maggie when I arrived, think about it... She looks as though she could be pretty special too.'

'I believe she also reads tea-leaves,' muttered Slane once Hattie had gone. 'Would you like a cognac or something with your coffee?' he asked, signalling for a waiter.

Maggie shook her head, sick with dread; she felt like running after the journalist and begging her to stay... but she couldn't put off the inevitable for ever. Though the irony was that she would have raised the subject herself had he not pre-empted her.

And now? The subject itself was one thing, but there was no way that she could bring herself to tell him the whole truth, she thought distractedly—that in a space of mere hours she had leapt from Peter's bed into his in the hope of salvaging—what? Her pride? Her self-confidence?

'I've asked them to order us a cab in a few minutes,' he said, his eyes coldly watchful as they met hers. 'So tell me, Maggie, what was your reason for so studiously avoiding any mention of our very first meeting?'

'I... I didn't think you'd remembered,' she stammered, raising her coffee-cup to her lips and almost dropping it as a strangulated noise escaped him.

'You what?' he choked, grabbing the cognac a waiter had just brought and taking a gulp of it. 'Pull the other leg, Maggie.'

'Well, you didn't say anything,' she retorted defensively, 'so how was I supposed to know?'

'You think I behave towards strangers the way I have to you?' he asked, his tone dripping sarcasm.

'I haven't the faintest idea how you behave to strangers; all I know—'

'Come now, Maggie; we were strangers one night almost three years ago.'

'You know perfectly well what I meant!' she

exclaimed, the colour leaping to her cheeks as a choking tightness gripped her throat.

'One thing that's always. . . I guess puzzled me is
why you took off the way you did,' he stated, his eyes
narrowed and unwaveringly watchful. 'I took a lot of
convincing, come the morning, that it hadn't all been a
dream.'

'I don't want to talk about it,' pleaded Maggie
hoarsely. 'No!' she insisted as he began to interject
angrily. 'We neither of us asked any questions then. . .
and you have no right to start asking them now!'

'Says who?' he drawled. 'Tell me, Maggie, just how
many guys have you left wondering if it hadn't all been
a beautiful dream?'

'Isn't that a question you should have asked three
years ago?' she said hoarsely, the viciousness of his
words reverberating through her like a thousand daggers. 'Or were you too busy kidding yourself that that
sort of behaviour was the exclusive prerogative of
males?'

For one terrifying moment she thought that he was
about to leap across the table at her in his fury, then
the waiter arrived to tell them that their taxi was
waiting.

It served him damned well right, she told herself as,
with a face like a thundercloud, he paid the bill and got
their coats.

She could fume all she liked about the double
standards applied to male and female sexuality, she
thought miserably as she followed her tight-lipped
companion out into the rain-lashed night—but somewhere along the line she had become conditioned by
them, otherwise she wouldn't have been left with the

feelings of unease that she had never been able to rid herself of concerning that night.

'I don't care what you say,' he growled once they were in the taxi. 'OK, if we'd run across one another at a social function or simply passed on the street we could have just left it. But hell, Maggie, we're working together—living in the same house. . . It's unreasonable not to talk about it!'

'I. . . Slane, it's all part of a period in my life I simply want to forget about,' she protested, the fact that she couldn't fault his argument making her feel all the worse.

'And to hell with the fact that it's also a part of my life!'

'You were the one who picked up a complete stranger!'

'Was I?' he demanded, his voice tight with fury. 'Well, I guess I didn't do too badly for a beginner.'

'You men and your double standards make me sick!' exploded Maggie, suddenly finding it all too much for her. 'You guess you didn't do too badly for a beginner! What's that supposed to mean—that you were a complete innocent I robbed of his virginity that night?'

'My, my,' he drawled. 'Where did Miss Prim go all of a sudden?'

'You know, that Hattie woman was wrong about you,' retorted Maggie witheringly. 'It's not so much a moralistic streak you have in you as one of self-righteous hypocrisy—and it's a mile wide.'

'Maybe you're right,' he muttered, digging in his jacket pocket for his wallet as the taxi drew up in front of the house, but he said no more.

Maggie leapt from the taxi with the intention of getting into the house and up to her room as quickly as she could — until she discovered that she hadn't brought a doorkey with her.

'Don't go running off. . .please, Maggie,' he said as he opened the door.

'What's the point?' she asked wearily. 'I don't want to discuss it — but you do. Can't you see we'll only end up saying things we'll both probably regret?'

'This guy you were in love with,' he stated flatly, completely ignoring her words, 'was he before or after me?'

'I. . . Slane, please. What's the point?' This guy she was in love with. . .she thought, with a jolt of apprehension. Now that really would take some explaining.

'Maggie, it matters to me.'

'He was. . .before you.'

She gave a start as he reached out and cupped her face gently in his hands, but she didn't resist — she was thinking about the lie she had just uttered.

'Maggie, why do you always jump when I touch you?' he whispered sadly.

'Because I'm afraid,' she burst out. Afraid because she had loved no one either before or after him, and afraid that if she loved anyone it was him.

'Of me — or of yourself?' he asked, releasing her. 'Or of men in general?'

'Slane, this isn't going to get us anywhere.'

'That only goes to show how little you know about masculine pride,' he countered drily.

'Masculine pride?'

'They always go on about hell having no fury like a woman scorned,' he drawled, 'but I'd say a woman scorned is a far safer bet than a man who's had his ego badly bruised.'

'My God, I. . .' Words failed her. Here she was,

tortured by a thousand ifs, buts and maybes and, worst of all, the growing conviction that she had somehow fallen in love with him, while all he was concerned about was his macho image!

'My God you what?'

'It's amazing what men are allowed to get away with in the name of their sacrosanct egos!' she exclaimed in disgust. 'I'm pretty sure that if you examined the cause of just about every war humankind has been subjected to you'd find some creep and his precious ego right there every time.'

'I think you and I should have a nightcap and discuss this,' Slane murmured with a wry smile, taking the coat she had just removed and hanging it with his on the hall stand. 'I'd hate to go down as the guy whose frail ego started the next world war.'

She was having second thoughts even as she followed him into the drawing room.

'What would you like to drink?' he asked.

'Something sweet. . .a Drambuie, a Cointreau. . . I don't mind.' She shouldn't be drinking anything, she told herself; she should have gone straight to her room. . .or, better still, she should never have come to Ireland in the first place.

'Midnight-blue,' he muttered, handing her the drink, but he said it so softly that she wasn't sure she had heard correctly. 'It accentuates your beauty.'

'Does it really?' she drawled, wondering what he hoped to gain by such insultingly transparent flattery.

'That's another thing that puzzles me about you, Maggie,' he stated, stretching himself out on the sofa opposite her chair. 'Your reaction to being told you're beautiful.'

'If I'm so beautiful how would you describe Felicity Field?'

'Oh, my God,' he sighed, grinning. 'I have a jealous woman on my hands!'

Maggie gave him her most withering look while studiously avoiding any examination of his joking statement.

'But to answer your question,' he continued, 'I'd say Felicity was no more than a very attractive woman—happy?'

'Delirious,' she retorted, then added wearily, 'Slane, don't you think it's about time we dropped these stupid games? Soon we'll be back in our respective homes and we'll be able to forget we ever met.'

'And that's what you want, is it—to be able to kid yourself we never met?' he demanded exasperatedly. 'Maggie, can't you see what you're doing to me? I keep getting the feeling that I've unknowingly committed some terrible crime against you, but—'

'Of course you haven't,' she gasped, disconcerted that he had even thought along such lines. 'Slane, I—' She broke off, her bemusement turning swiftly to anger. 'Make up your mind—a few moments ago it was your bruised ego you were complaining about.'

'And I could probably come up with half a dozen more points—all perfectly valid—that bug me about your attitude towards me,' he retorted sharply. 'And, as for your earlier gibe about double standards, who the hell am I to judge how others choose to lead their lives?

'When I met you three years ago I have to admit I was in a pretty screwed-up state. . .but it seemed pretty plain to me that you were in a very similar state yourself that night. Or did I imagine that?'

'No,' said Maggie huskily, 'you didn't imagine it.' What point was there in denying it?'

'I got over the state I was in,' he said quietly, 'but I'm pretty certain you haven't. If you had you wouldn't be having the problems you're having now even mentioning the subject.' He took a sip from his glass. 'Maggie, are you ashamed of what happened between us?'

'I... I probably was for a while,' she stammered, caught off guard.

'For a while?' he murmured, an edge of scepticism in his tone. 'Did you feel you'd been unfaithful to him?'

'I—No!' she exploded, repugnance shuddering through her as her mind inexplicably filled with a vision of Peter Francomb. 'I wasn't being unfaithful to anyone! Why can't you just accept that what happened simply happened?'

'And you taking off without so much as a word— that simply happened too?'

'That's your whole problem, isn't it?' she snapped, spilling some of her drink in her agitation. 'The fact that I had the gall to leap from your bed without so much as a thank-you!'

She hadn't seen him move but suddenly he was standing before her, his face an expressionless mask as he handed her a handkerchief with which to mop up the spilt drink.

'Yeah—that's my whole problem,' he drawled. 'And what's yours, Maggie?' With an exclamation of impatience he removed her glass from her and deposited it on the small table beside her chair, then took the handkerchief from her and wiped the drink from the front of her dress.

'At least the girl who shared my only experience of

a one-night stand had a bit of chutzpah about her,' he accused quietly. 'I liked her enough to be upset to see what she's turned into.'

'Perhaps she grew up and decided one-night stands weren't going to get her anywhere,' retorted Maggie defiantly, and felt weak as she unaccountably found herself imagining her mother's reaction to this picture that she was so recklessly painting of herself.

'So now you've switched to crawling into this Miss Prim shell every time a guy touches you. . .in an attempt to keep yourself faithful to some guy who's no longer in your life?'

'Yes!' At least her poor mother would find that preferable to the idea of her only daughter prowling the streets like a predatory avenger, she thought weakly.

'But why?' he demanded, yanking her to her feet and half into his arms. 'By your crazy reckoning you've already been unfaithful to him,' he whispered hoarsely, his arms drawing her against him, 'and you still are, even if so far it's only in thought.'

'Yes, fine. . .you're absolutely right,' muttered Maggie from between tightly clenched teeth as he buried his face against her hair.

Fighting the heady sensations already threatening to overwhelm her, she cast aside all thought of her mother and tried to distract herself by silently cursing her inexplicable bout of tears earlier. She could hardly blame him for what he had read into her tears, but they had landed her with his having become fixated on the ludicrous idea of her remaining faithful to a fictitious, long-lost lover.

Suddenly she felt close to panic, knowing that if she moved so much as a muscle she would give in to the terrible need now almost tearing her apart, not simply to welcome him into her arms but to feel the power his body had once given hers filling her again.

'Does that satisfy your bruised ego enough?' she added vindictively.

He lifted his head and laughed softly when she turned hers from the disturbing darkness in his eyes. 'No, that doesn't satisfy it in the least.' He shook her in gentle exasperation. 'Not looking at me isn't going to help,' he mocked huskily. 'I can feel your heart beating—I can't tell which is going faster, yours or mine.'

'Just because I still find you attractive it doesn't mean—Slane, please. . .stop this!'

'Why, Maggie?' he demanded harshly. 'You're free, even though you kid yourself you're not, and you want me as much as I want you. . .so give me one good reason why I should stop.'

'What about your ego?' she asked unsteadily. 'Can it cope with knowing how I feel?'

'Exactly how *do* you feel, Maggie?' he whispered, his mouth lowering to brush softly against hers, then crushing hungrily down on hers as it met with not the slightest resistance.

It was like coming home, she thought incredulously as she lifted her arms and clung to him, her body rejoicing in the swift surge of desire it encountered in his with an abandon that brought a soft groan bursting from him. And when he began drawing away from her her impassioned resistance brought another groan— almost of pain—from him as he forced her from him and held her at arm's length.

'No,' he protested hoarsely, his eyes refusing to meet hers. 'This won't work! We hardly know any more about one another than we did last time.' He turned from her and strode towards the door.

'In other words,' hurled Maggie after him, feeling as though she had just been doused in freezing water, 'your fragile ego simply can't take it!' She almost fell back onto the chair behind her, unable to believe she had actually uttered those taunting words.

'Yeah—I guess that's about it,' he drawled from the doorway. 'But don't you fret any, Maggie; I'm sure I'll find some way round it.'

CHAPTER SEVEN

'MAGGIE, would you like me to make you another cup of coffee—or tea, perhaps?'

'Slane, to say you're beginning to get on my nerves would be a gross understatement,' groaned Maggie, an underlying amusement in her exasperated tone.

'I guess you're just edgy,' he murmured with cloying solicitude, then cursed ripely as he knocked over a phial he had just prepared. 'And I'm clumsy,' he sighed. 'It's interesting how a night of sleepless frustration can affect two people so differently.'

'What's so interesting about it?' enquired Maggie, glancing across at him as he started cleaning up the mess he had made and giving a silent groan of protest as her head became filled with erotic memories—the same memories that had tormented her throughout the entire night.

'So you're not denying the kind of night you had,' he observed smugly.

'Slane, how am I supposed to work with you wittering on so irritatingly?' she protested.

'You really do know how to boost a guy's morale,' he sighed with pious indignation. 'All I'm doing is being my natural, sociable self. You obviously don't realise how deeply hurt I was yesterday to learn that you thought I always behaved the way I had with you. . . So which is it to be—tea or coffee?'

'Slane!'

'Maggie, this isn't going to work if you keep hollering at me like that.'

'What isn't going to work?'

'My acting like a regular guy towards you.'

'Slane, if your acting like "a regular guy", as you put it, entails your interrupting me every five seconds with offers of coffee—'

'Or tea,' he cut in with relentless brightness. 'I can just as easily do you some tea.'

'I think I'd prefer it if you returned to your former irregular self,' Maggie ploughed on, undeterred.

It had started when, worn out and tense after a night without sleep, she had entered the kitchen that morning to be ushered to the table and served eggs scrambled to perfection, coffee and toast.

By the time she had been handed her coat and solicitously helped into the car, both her curiosity and her sense of humour had been well and truly stimulated. It was all so tongue-in-cheek that she hadn't the slightest doubt that there was nothing in the least genuine about this sudden change in him... It was the motive behind the change that both intrigued and worried her.

'I'll do a deal with you,' he said, with a grin. 'I'll drop my candidate-for-a-sainthood routine if you promise to kick this other guy right out of your mind every time he appears in it.'

'Slane, for heaven's sake—'

'For heaven's sake nothing,' he protested. 'Maggie, it just occurred to me this morning that we have little more than a week left here together... All I want is for us to be able to part friends—well, that and you leaving minus this hang-up you have about men. Is that too much to ask?'

Maggie broke off from what she was doing, staggered by the effect that the idea of leaving was having on her.

'Who says I have a hang-up about men?' she muttered, almost absent-mindedly. All he wanted was for them to part as friends, she thought wryly. And she had planted this ridiculous idea in his head of her pining for some long-lost lover because. . .because the sort of truth she had to tell was something she couldn't bring herself to divulge to the man with whom she was rapidly falling in love.

'Stop trying to pick a fight,' he retorted, reaching over and cuffing her gently on the cheek. 'And stop fretting over whether or not I'm trying to lure you back into my bed—because I am.'

Maggie's eyes widened, then she burst out laughing.

Slane's eyes also widened, and for a brief instant his mouth dropped open, then he too started laughing.

'But for strictly therapeutic reasons,' chuckled Maggie. 'Is that what you're saying?'

'It's good to see you laugh like that,' he said quietly. 'In fact, so good that I'd happily renounce all bed-related intentions just to know you'll keep on laughing like that once you've left here.'

Maggie flashed him a startled look, silently cursing the lie that had inspired him with this alarming determination to rehabilitate her, and feeling even more alarmed by the realisation of how little like laughing she was going to feel once he was out of her life.

'Yes, I know I'm sounding almost too good to be true,' he said, grinning, 'but your ghosts and mine have somehow become linked, so I'm not being entirely altruistic in this.'

Maggie made a show of being engrossed in what she

was doing. 'And how's that?' she eventually asked unconcernedly.

'The last time I saw Marjorie was the day after you and I ran into each other. My mother and I came over here for her funeral, but I'd never been back until now... And I've never been back to England either, since that wedding—' He broke off with an exclamation of impatience. 'I'm sorry—this can't be making any sense to you.'

'Of course it makes sense to me,' said Maggie quietly. 'You lost two people you loved dearly in a very short space of time. You must have dreaded coming here, knowing Marjorie wouldn't be around. And as for England—given the circumstances under which you last went there, I can understand perfectly well why you wouldn't be in a hurry to return there unless you had to.'

'You make it sound so reasonable,' he muttered, 'except that really it isn't any more reasonable than your being indoctrinated with the idea that you're only allowed one chance at love.'

Maggie closed her eyes. This was getting completely out of hand, she thought frustratedly. But how could she extricate herself, when she was the one who had planted the idea in him in the first place?

'Slane, I... I know my attitude isn't right.'

'Yes, but you haven't been the one preaching about putting the past behind you,' he sighed. 'If I've been such a success at it, how come it's taken me all this time to return here? I wasn't being completely honest when I said it was because of Marjorie that I put off coming back—though of course she had a lot to do with it...

'It was only when I walked into Connor's house and

saw you there that it all came back to me and I realised
that I've still not properly come to terms with the way
I behaved after my father's death.'

'Why should seeing me have made you think that?'
asked Maggie, every nerve in her crying out to put her
arms around him in comfort.

'Because, like everything else about that time, I'd
pushed you out of my mind. But seeing you again was
like being hurled back in time. . .feeling the same
feelings and hurting the same hurts—' He broke off to
measure out a solution.

'I guess that was why I felt so defensive when I spoke
with Connor, knowing what would be going through
his mind. Of course I'm doing this because of my dad,
but I wouldn't have become this personally involved if
it had been anyone other than Maurice who'd set it up.
And I owe you an apology—I had no right to take all
this out on you but I have been, and I truly am sorry.'

'Slane, have you nearly finished that batch?' asked
Maggie, a sudden briskness in her tone.

'Another couple of minutes,' he replied, giving her a
slightly startled look then glancing at his watch. 'I also
apologise for all this introspection; it must be boring
the pants off you. . . But to make up for it I'll help you
finish off yours, then we can knock off for the day.'

'I wasn't in the least bored,' replied Maggie, her
heart thudding. 'I just thought it would be nice to have
a walk on our way home—along that lovely beach we
always pass.'

'It's dark, cold and bucketing down with rain—and
you want to walk along a beach?' he groaned in
disbelief.

'That's right,' she laughed. 'As you said, we've only
just over a week left, and with the amount of sorting

out of one another we have to get through in that time
I think we might as well start out with clear heads.'

'So you reckon I need sorting out too, do you?' he
murmured, flashing her a grin that sent her heart
spinning.

'We'll discuss that when we've finished this work,'
she replied primly, 'so I suggest you get on with it.'

There was a part of Maggie that kept on begging her
to slow down, think things through, but it was as though
the rest of her was on a beautiful high. She knew that
she wasn't behaving rationally, but for the past three
years she had managed to overrationalise her life
almost out of existence.

It had been just that one flash of vulnerability that
he had betrayed, and the knowledge that this was one
area in which she could help, that had triggered off this
feeling in her and left her feeling as though a terrible
weight had been lifted from her.

'I've a good mind to let you get out and open the
gate,' he muttered as they drew up in front of it with
him at the wheel, 'because we'll both be soaked to the
skin once we've been on that beach for a few seconds—
Hey, I didn't mean it!' he yelled as Maggie leapt from
the car.

At least she could stop pretending to herself that she
wasn't sure whether or not she loved him, she thought
as she dragged open the heavy gates, then saluted as
he drove through, shaking a fist at her.

'Maggie, what's gotten into you?' he demanded when
she leapt back in.

'I'm perfectly capable of opening a couple of gates,'
she laughed.

'It's what else you're capable of that's beginning to

worry me,' he chuckled, turning his gaze from the road to glance at her. 'And you still haven't told me what's gotten into you.'

'I'll tell you while we're walking.'

'Dear God,' he groaned, 'the woman really is serious about this darned walk. Couldn't I just sit in the car and watch you?'

'Then you'll never know what's got—sorry, *gotten*—into me,' she teased.

He was still protesting volubly when he pulled the car over onto a verge by the beach and switched off the engine.

'What if I told you I had handmade shoes on?' he enquired tentatively.

'Well, even though I can't make any such claims about mine, I intended taking them off anyway—so I suggest you do the same.'

'But my socks will get wet and sandy,' he protested as she began taking off her shoes.

'Stop being such a wimp,' she laughed while discreetly easing her dress up under her raincoat prior to removing the tights she had forgotten she would have to contend with.

'Excuse me, Maggie,' he said in a shocked tone, 'but what are you doing?'

'Taking off my tights,' she retorted.

'Oh, my God—my reputation!' he groaned, contorting his body to remove his shoes. 'You know what's going to happen any second now? Hattie Lang's going to appear from the bushes with a couple of photographers and—'

'Get your socks off and roll up your trousers,' laughed Maggie as she finished removing her tights then opened the door.

'Sorry—which was it I was to get off?' he called as she jumped out of the car and almost out of her skin as the wind lashed freezing rain round her bare legs.

Perhaps this *was* pretty drastic, she thought as she raised the collar of her coat and walked gingerly across the spiky grass and onto the beach, but she needed a blast of fresh air to clear her head. And air didn't come any fresher than this, she told herself as she reached the sand and found herself almost running along the beach with the force of the wind buffeting her in the back.

'Hey, you said a walk!' yelled Slane, catching up with her and taking her by the arm to slow her down. 'If I catch cold out here I'll expect you to nurse me through it and, I promise you, I make a lousy patient.'

'That I can believe,' she laughed, feeling as wild and free as the weather. 'But anyway the common cold, being a virus, can't be brought on by—'

'I can't hear you!'

'I said the—Oh, forget it.'

'What?' he yelled, then gave a roar of protest as the heavens opened on them. Turning her to face him, he cupped his hands against her ear and bellowed down it, 'Now do you give up?'

She nodded vigorously—a movement that sent rain trickling down the back of her neck. Laughing, he grabbed her hand as they turned to make back for the car. It was only now that she was having to walk against the wind that Maggie realised its true strength, and when Slane slipped a supportive arm around her she found herself hanging onto him for all she was worth.

'If we ever go for a walk again,' he groaned once they were back in the car, 'it will be at a time and a place of *my* choosing. God, I must have been out of my mind to listen to you!'

'It seemed like a good idea at the time,' said Maggie, shivering, feeling cold and suddenly deflated. What on earth had possessed her?

'But one thing's for sure—if our heads aren't clear enough now to start this sorting out you were talking about, they never will be,' he chuckled, dusting off his feet and putting his shoes and socks back on.

Maggie closed her eyes and leaned her head back. And another thing that was for sure, she thought wearily, was that she was beyond being sorted out.

Come the end of this two-week period she was going to be devastated beyond imagining—and there she had been, cavorting around a beach, full of the joys of spring, telling herself that she was in love...in love with a man who looked forward not only to their parting in friendship, but to her being free of what he mistakenly believed to be her hang-ups over men, so that she could form new relationships!

'I can feel you slipping away from me,' he chided softly, reaching out and tracing his forefinger down the side of her face. 'Don't you feel I'm worth sorting out any more?'

'Of course you are,' she retorted huskily, resisting an urge to catch his hand and draw it back to her as he removed it. 'But sometimes I get these spur-of-the-moment feelings when everything seems so clear—then later—'

'Look, the walk wasn't such a bad idea—it's just that the timing was lousy,' he protested.

'I didn't mean that,' said Maggie. 'It was when you told me how you reacted to seeing me... All sorts of things used to make me react like that at first, and still do at times, though mercifully rarely now—and my father's been gone for six years.'

'I'm not sure what you're saying, Maggie,' he said quictly.

'Neither am I,' she sighed. 'It's just that when you said that seeing me brought back your guilt over the way you'd behaved it reminded me of all the ways I used to avoid the central issue—my father's death. At first I was terrified of grieving openly, for fear of upsetting my mother even more than she already was... Then somewhere along the line my ability to express my grief became impaired and I ended up taking it out on my mother and Jim.

'I think what I'm trying to say is that you met me very soon after losing your father, and it was more your feelings of loss over him that you were reliving... Oh, God, I haven't the right to be talking like this!'

'I happen to think you're talking a lot of sense,' he stated quietly. 'The only reason I was able to come here was because I'd arranged to have a couple of weeks off after a pretty gruelling two months—but my actual decision to come here was completely spur-of-the-moment.

'I was already feeling tired and disorientated and more than a little apprehensive when I walked in and saw you.. .so I guess my reactions weren't too logical— and I can only apologise for the way I behaved towards you.'

He gave a sudden shiver and started up the car. 'I don't know about you, but I need a long soak in a very hot tub.'

'A very long soak,' agreed Maggie, by now feeling utterly deflated.

'It sounds as though you did the sensible thing and had counselling at some point,' he said a while later.

'I'm afraid not. I just happened to share digs for a while with a girl who was reading psychology—part of her course dealt with bereavement counselling and she used me as a guinea pig. I only wish I'd run into someone like her a couple of years earlier.'

'Before you'd started working it all out for yourself?' he enquired perceptively.

Maggie gave him a startled look. 'Yes,' she agreed with a sigh. 'Jim and I even managed to have a laugh over the terminology used in the textbooks, when I told him about it. By then I'd aleady mended my fences with him and my mother and had begun staying with them during the holidays.'

'But it was to Connor rather than Jim that you turned when you needed a father figure,' he observed quietly.

Maggie shook her head vehemently. 'No. Jim was fantastic. . . He acted exactly as my father would have, though heaven only knows how he managed to after the way I'd treated him for so long.'

After fleeing Brighton she had arrived on her mother and stepfather's doorstep on the verge of collapse, only to find that her mother had left to take an elderly neighbour to the doctor. When Jim had opened the door and seen her distraught state he had hesitated only momentarily before putting his arms round her and bundling her inside. She had poured it all out to him—all about Peter; she had never told a living soul about Slane.

'It was just that it all happened during term-time. . . and all Connor did was take over from Jim. I—' She broke off with a muffled gasp as it suddenly dawned on her that she was gabbling on as though he knew what she was talking about. 'I. . . I suppose I was just lucky to have two such wonderful surrogate fathers when I needed them.'

'It's all right, Maggie,' he reassured her gently; 'I'm not about to cross-examine you.'

She said nothing, her thoughts drifting into wondering what his reaction would be to the real truth. She was the one with all the hang-ups about actually admitting that within hours of losing her virginity to one man she had spent a night of unbridled passion with another. . . Now she had become embroiled in such a string of lies that she could barely think straight.

'There's a delicatessen over there,' he muttered, drawing the car to a halt. 'Let's go see what they have—it would save us cooking.

'Good idea,' said Maggie, 'but, if you don't mind, you go—I haven't got my shoes on and, anyway, I've seized up.'

'That'll teach you not to go running along beaches in gales in your bare feet,' he murmured, grinning wickedly at her before getting out of the car.

Why, she wondered miserably as she dusted the sand from her feet and watched his tall figure cross the road, hadn't she known that first time that she was going to end up loving him like this?

And as for this pack of lies she had become so enmeshed in, it didn't really matter what he thought of her—by the end of next week he would be out of her life for good. . .and, if Hattie Lang was to be believed, straight back into the life of someone like Felicity Field.

'It's not a good idea sending me out shopping when I'm hungry,' complained Slane as, having placed a couple of carrier bags on the back seat, he got back into the car. 'It took a good deal of will-power on my part not to buy up half the store.'

'So what did you get?' asked Maggie, deciding it was little wonder that she was having such problems even thinking coherently when she was in this crazy situation of playing house with this dish of a man with whom she was falling head over heels in love.

'Well, I'd picked out a whole load of things,' he replied as he started up the car, 'but then this beautiful aroma hit me—home-made vegetable broth. So I settled for a pail of that, together with some freshly baked bread. . .and, a few slices of ham. Then there was this chocolate cake and—'

'I wish I'd never asked,' she laughed, love spreading through her and filling her with a soft, melting warmth.

'It won't take too long to heat up the broth and make some ham sandwiches once we've bathed,' he said, glancing across at her. 'Have you thawed out any yet?'

'A little—but I still can't wait to get into that bath.'

'I'll light a fire in the study and we can eat round that,' he said, then chuckled. 'Perhaps you'd like to go for another walk after we've eaten?'

'Maggie! It's for you!'

Maggie had just finished drying her hair and switched off the dryer when Slane's bellowed words reached her. If it was the telephone she hadn't even heard it ring, she thought, belting her bathrobe tightly around her and flying down the stairs to the study.

A robed Slane was on his knees before the fireplace.

'Sorry about the phone,' he muttered, turning towards her with a grin and waving sooty hands at her.

She realised what he meant the instant she picked up the receiver—it was covered in coal dust.

'Mum!' she exclaimed on hearing her mother's voice. 'What's wrong?'

'Why on earth should anything be wrong, darling?' protested her mother. 'I just thought I'd ring and see how you're getting on with your laboratory work.'

'Fine, though it's not exactly scintillating,' she replied. 'How are you and Jim?'

'Thriving. Jim sends his love, but he's soaking in the bath at the moment. I take it that was your American scientist who answered the phone. Is he also staying at Connor's house?'

'Actually, he is,' chuckled Maggie, detecting a note of interest in her mother's tone. 'The scientist turned out to be Connor's cousin, Slane,' she added, pretty sure that the name would mean nothing to her mother.

'Slane? What a strange name... It's funny how deceptive voices can be; he actually sounded a lot younger than Connor.'

'I must tell him that—he'll be pleased,' murmured Maggie, not feeling the slightest trace of guilt at the deception. Any man around Slane's age was eligible as far as her mother was concerned; the fact that he might still be in the room wouldn't deter her in the least from demanding a detailed description of him.

'Did I tell you that poor Mr Barry next door broke his leg?'

Slane had the fire going nicely by the time Maggie's mother had related every detail of the saga of Mr Barry's leg, and she had moved onto the dreadfulness of the weather when he mimed that he was going to clean himself up and start the supper.

'Anyway, it was lovely talking to you, darling, but I'd

better get back to doing the supper. Take care and we're both looking forward to seeing you soon.'

'You take care too—and love to Jim.'

She raced to the kitchen once she had replaced the receiver, and found Slane with the sandwiches made and the broth simmering on the cooker.

'I feel dreadful about leaving you to do all that,' she said apologetically. 'I'll do all the clearing up after—and make the coffee.'

'Are you sure you're not related to my mother?' he enquired with a lazy grin. 'Anyway, make yourself useful now that you're here—does Connor have any trays?'

'Yes. In that cupboard next to the fridge. Is there time for me to nip upstairs quickly and get dressed?' she asked, suddenly aware of the fact that she hadn't a stitch on under her robe.

'No, there darned well isn't!' he exclaimed. 'Anyway, you're as dressed as I am... Now what are you doing?' he groaned as Maggie went over to the sink.

'At least let me wash my hands,' she protested. 'There was coal dust all over the receiver.'

'Well, I'll go see to that, ma'am,' he murmured, 'just as soon as I've finished my chores here.'

'Sorry, sorry, sorry,' chanted Maggie, drying her hands and getting out the trays. 'I promise you won't have to lift so much as another finger for the entire evening.'

'So what was it you had to tell me?' he asked, ladling broth into the bowls.

'I can't remember having to tell you anything,' she said, puzzled, and placed the sandwiches on a plate.

'You told your mother you'd have to tell me whatever it was—and that I'd be pleased.'

'You shouldn't eavesdrop,' she protested indignantly, colour rising in her cheeks at the memory of her deception.

'You're blushing, Maggie.'

'As you've worked yourself to death, you go into the study and I'll bring your tray in,' she said, doggedly ignoring his teasing words. Why was it that he always seemed to home in on anything even approaching a lie on her part?

'I'l carry in my own tray,' he laughed, 'and we can finish this intriguing conversation in front of the fire.'

'All right, all right, I'll explain,' she groaned as he turned to her, his expression the epitome of rapt expectancy, once they were seated around the fire with their trays on their laps. 'My mother happened to remark that your voice sounded a lot younger than Connor's. . .and I told her that you'd be pleased to hear it.'

'You're darned right I am—I'm thirty-odd years younger than the guy!' He tilted his head to one side, examining her intently. 'Is that it?'

Maggie nodded unconcernedly.

'Come to think of it, eavesdropping intently though I was, I don't seem to recall any mention having been made of my true age.' He began chuckling softly.

'Drink your soup before it gets cold,' she murmured, and took a bite out of a sandwich. 'Mmm—this is delicious!'

'Don't talk with your mouth full,' he growled, still chuckling. 'So you decided to let your mom think you were house-sharing with a guy pushing seventy, did you?'

'Thank your lucky stars I did,' retorted Maggie, her mouth once again full, 'because if I hadn't I'd still be on the phone to her now—giving weight, height, shoe size, eye colour and every other detail imaginable.'

'Is that so?' he murmured, then added, 'Well, now you can stop yacking and eat.'

Maggie was about to protest that she had only been answering his question—but decided not to bother—the food was delicious and the heat from the fire was bliss.

'I'm afraid I couldn't look at chocolate cake, so you can have both slices,' she told him when they had finished and she was clearing the trays.

'I couldn't look at it either,' he said, grinning, 'so we'll have it for breakfast.'

She had just finished stacking the dishwasher when she heard the telephone ring and flew back to the study.

'Just ask me anything you like,' Slane was saying into the mouthpiece. 'My shoe size, my weight—Hey!' he yelled as the receiver was snatched from him.

'Look, Mum, that was. . . Connor?'

'Did I hear that young devil aright?' demanded the professor. 'Why would he think I'd be interested—?'

'It's his pathetic idea of a joke,' cut in Maggie, flashing Slane a murderous look as he tried to take the receiver back from her. 'How are you?' she asked, trying to shoulder aside Slane, who had virtually draped himself around her in his determination not to miss a word.

'Great. I've been catching up on the gossip here and running into colleagues I haven't seen for years. So how are you two getting on?'

'Not too well, I'm afraid,' butted in Slane, his head now clamped against Maggie's. 'I'm worn out doing all the cooking.'

'Good—I had an idea she'd keep you in your place,' chuckled Connor. 'How's the testing coming along?'

'No problems,' replied Slane, wrapping an arm round Maggie and almost throttling her in his attempts to stop her struggling. 'Mind you, Maggie just stands around making coffee while I—'

'Connor, you know that isn't true,' she cut in indignantly as she tried to elbow Slane in the ribs.

'Damn it, which one of you is on the line?' demanded the professor.

'We both are,' replied Slane. 'Remember how I always said you needed a few telephone extensions around the place?' he chuckled. 'Well, now you have one in every room. I'm speaking to you from the hallway and I believe Maggie's on the kitchen extension.'

'Maggie—what's he been up to?'

'Nothing, I promise,' she said, her words distorted by her sharp intake of breath as Slane crossed his arms around her and drew her back against him.

'Well, I see there was no point in my worrying about whether or not the pair of you were getting on,' he observed archly. 'Slane, I've been in touch with your mother. She and I are off to the opera on Saturday and then we'll be. . .'

Maggie could still hear his voice, but she was no longer capable of taking in the words as her body began responding with mind-blowing excitement to the feel of Slane's.

'Yes, great—enjoy the rest of your visit and give Mom my love,' Slane was saying. 'Yes, she's still here.' He butted her head gently with his. 'Wake up—Connor wants to say goodbye to you.'

'Maggie, you take care of yourself, darling,' ordered

Connor's jovial tones, 'and don't be letting Slane bully you. I'll be over in London soon after I get back, so I'll see you then.'

It was Slane who took the receiver from her hand and replaced it on its cradle. Then he returned his hand to where it had been and stood there, rocking gently on his heels, his cheek pressed against hers. With the rest of his body also pressed against hers there was no mistaking the fierceness of the need in him, and as she leaned her head back against him in silent acquiescence Maggie felt only relief that it matched hers.

'All of a sudden I'm afraid to say anything,' he whispered huskily, his lips nuzzling against her ear.

'I'm the one with the things to say,' she said, shivering, trying desperately to rein in some rational thoughts. 'I should have explained—'

'No!' he protested hoarsely. 'We didn't need words before. . .we don't need them now.' He undid the belt of her robe, a softly groaned sigh escaping him as his hands discovered her nakedness. 'Do you remember, Maggie?' he whispered as his hands cupped her breasts. 'Oh, yes—you remember,' he chuckled softly as her flesh strained and hardened beneath the caressing touch of his fingers.

She made a soft sound of protest as she tried to turn in his arms, wanting to experience the never-forgotten feel of her own around him, and felt him resist.

'I want to hold you,' she protested, raising her arms up and behind her, turning her own head as she drew his to her.

'I've waited too long for this,' he breathed against her parted lips. 'I wouldn't be able to stop if I let you turn now and we wouldn't be protected. But I'm darned if I know how we're going to get up those stairs,' he groaned, his mouth hungrily claiming hers.

Their journey to his room was a protracted, tortuous procedure that was in danger of being abandoned on several occasions. When they at last reached it they fell on one another in a breathless frenzy of need, casting aside their robes in a desperate orgy of touching and exploring as though fearful that this magical moment of rediscovery might suddenly be snatched from them.

'If you promise not to run away from me I'll let go of you,' he whispered unsteadily, drawing her head away from his and gazing down at her with eyes hot with desire.

'I don't want you to let go of me,' she confessed distractedly, then tensed as laughter rippled through the exquisitely sculptured body to which hers clung in blatant need.

Her laughter momentarily joined his when he suddenly fell backwards onto the bed, carrying her with him, their bodies still suffocatingly entwined.

He rolled over, turning her onto her back, his eyes glittering down into hers as he drew her arms from around him and held them trapped against the bed. Then he lowered his head till his lips were brushing softly against the engorged tip of first one then the other of her breasts. Back and forth he moved between each, his lips, his tongue and his teeth punishing her straining flesh with remembered pleasures so exquisite that cries of protest began exploding from her.

'I'm trying not to let you rush me,' he groaned, barely coherently.

'Why?' she cried out.

'I guess I'm also trying to kid myself I'm not out of control,' he sighed, releasing her wrists and sliding his hands up her arms then down her body, a soft, shuddering groan whispering from him as she wound her arms around his neck while her body arched urgently against his, driven by the hot waves of a terrible need now pounding through her.

'No!' she gasped incredulously when he suddenly sat up and turned away from her.

'I've stopped kidding myself about being in control...but I'm not about to run away,' he protested unsteadily when she rose and flung herself against his back. He reached for her hand and guided it to what he was doing. She pressed her mouth against the bronzed smoothness of his back, tasting the salty sweetness of his skin and biting back a flood of words of love.

When he returned to her arms all those words broke loose, only to be lost in the passionate hunger of his mouth on hers, and within seconds she was crying out in elation as her body welcomed the explosive power of his. Then her cries began melting into soft sobs of incoherency as she felt herself disintegrate into a million atoms of pleasure.

'I thought my memories were all exaggerated,' she protested wildly, laughter and pleasure dancing through her words.

'And weren't they?' he chuckled raggedly, the urgent rhythm of his body within hers slowing and deepening.

'They were a gross underestimation,' she groaned distractedly, clasping his head and planting feverish kisses on his face as her body once more ran devastatingly out of control.

Later, when that sweet devastation began manifesting itself yet again, it brought with it a perceptibly heightened tension, a fiercer, more demanding urgency in the gleaming body that was wreaking such mind-blowing pleasure on hers.

'Oh, God—what are you doing to me?' There was laughter and exultation in his question, cried out in that sublime moment before the world halted, then exploded around them.

For several minutes they lay spent in one another's arms, while their starved lungs replenished themselves. Then, displaying reserves of energy that left Maggie limp with disbelief, Slane embarked on the laborious task of extracting the quilt from beneath them, pausing every now and then to plant the odd kiss or two on whatever part of her that happened to be in line with his mouth, then flung it over them.

'You forgot to plump up the pillows,' she teased lazily, sensations of joy almost suffocating her as one of those random kisses landed on her chin.

'God, but you're the ungrateful woman,' he growled in pure brogue, then slid himself down the bed and cushioned his head against her breasts. 'Do what you like to your pillow,' he chuckled, 'but leave mine alone—it's perfect.'

She felt as if her heart was about to burst with happiness as she curved her arms around his head and ran her fingers lazily through his hair. She felt that she could hear the heavy pounding of her heart, and wondered why he wasn't complaining of its deafening noise.

'No regrets?' he asked softly.

'None,' she replied dreamily.

'So, you see, it wasn't such a wise move on your part—running away from me that first time.'

'How do you mean?' asked Maggie, the breath becoming trapped in her lungs.

'You didn't stay long enough for me to help lay your ghost.'

'Slane, I have to explain about—'

'You don't have to explain anything. All I ask is that when the time comes for me to pack you off to London you'll have laid him to rest once and for all.'

Her fingers resumed their rhythmic stroking of his hair, but inwardly she was falling apart. In the euphoria brought about by their lovemaking she had entered a fool's paradise... All he wanted was to set her free to love; all she wanted was *his* love.

And now her pack of lies were about to become true, she reflected bitterly. She had actually thought it ludicrous—the idea of loving one, unattainable man to the exclusion of all others... Now it didn't seem in the least ludicrous.

CHAPTER EIGHT

MAGGIE remembered a lot of things during that tempestuous night that it had never occurred to her that she knew about Slane. Though the ardour which had stripped her of her every inhibition had always remained with her, it puzzled her that she could ever have forgotten the zany humour that he was liable, without warning, to introduce into lovemaking. When she later found herself wondering how many other women had shared that side of him, she felt the knot of misery within her tighten even more painfully.

'Maggie, are you awake?' he enquired drowsily, his head stirring on the pillow of her breasts to which it had returned time and again during the night.

'Mmm.' Misery was swiftly nudged aside by joyous elation as she hugged his head to her.

'I have some instructions for you,' he said. 'Instructions which I want you to follow with absolute precision and without a word of question—understood?'

'Understood, sir,' she giggled.

'Stop jiggling around like that!'

'Sorry. . .sir.'

'I'm not joking,' he growled, sandpapering her warningly with his chin.

'Neither am I,' she laughed. 'I'm awaiting your instructions.'

'Right. I am about to lift my head from your person.'

'From my what?'

'Maggie! And when I do so you are to roll right—and I do mean right—away from me.'

'Right—not left?'

'Maggie!'

He lifted his head from her and, as so precisely instructed, she rolled away from him. He leapt from the bed.

'No!' he roared as she made to turn to see what he was up to. 'Stay right where you are and don't move!'

'Perhaps I should have sneaked away in the night again,' she choked weakly, 'before you turned into a despot.'

'I've already tried to escape from that bed once this morning, so how else do you think I was going to get out of the damned thing without you making more demands on me?' he demanded indignantly. 'I am now going to shower my battered, exhausted person, after which, if I have the strength, I shall stagger down the stairs to prepare your breakfast.'

'Slane, I—'

'Chocolate cake and cream!' came his laughing voice from the hallway.

Maggie gathered herself and part of her wits together and took them off to the second bathroom. Under the shower she cried her heart out.

She dried herself and got dressed, mulling hopelessly over the fact that she had landed herself in the no-win situation to end them all. Embarking on an affair—destined to last little more than a week—with a man whose feelings for her boiled down to nothing deeper than wishing her well was as plain a recipe for disaster as any she could imagine.

She was the one who had turned to a stranger in the bizarre hope that sex with no commitment would somehow miraculously cure her woes. . .so who was she to argue with that stranger now, when he was only continuing what had been started three years ago?

She gave a start as she heard what sounded like a gong being struck. It clanged twice more before she reached the top of the stairs.

'Madam's breakfast is ready.' Slane grinned up at her from the foot of the stairs, brass gong in hand. 'And if madam doesn't get her ass down here right now—'

'Where on earth did you get that thing?' laughed Maggie, running downstairs, and she suddenly knew that it was pointless seeking a rational explanation for her behaviour. A lifetime, a week or only an hour— whatever her time with him was to be she would live every last second of it to the hilt because that, it appeared, was the way she was.

'Great, isn't it?' he chuckled, placing the ornate brass contraption on the hall table. 'I found it in the dining room. Marjorie got this when I was just a kid—said it saved her hollering herself hoarse getting Connor and me to the meal table.'

Maggie smiled up at him, her heart brimming over with love.

He took a couple of exaggerated steps back from her. 'Just you keep your distance, young lady,' he warned, with a grin. 'We have a day's work ahead of us—so no shenanigans!'

'So that's what shenanigans are,' she murmured, following him into the kitchen. 'I. . . Oh, no!' she groaned as she caught sight of the table, and the two massive portions of chocolate cake neatly set out with a jug of cream to accompany them. 'Slane, I thought you were joking!'

'I never joke about a subject as serious as food,' he informed her primly, then chuckled. 'OK—sling it back in the icebox and I'll see what I can come up with.'

By the time Maggie had returned from the fridge boiled eggs and a rack of toast had appeared on the table.

'This is wonderful!' she exclaimed, and began pouring them both coffee.

'Yes, but it'll have to stop,' he sighed. 'I can't send you out into the world believing your average guy will be willing to serve you up meals the way I do—let alone be capable of doing so.'

Maggie forced a smile to her lips as she felt a thousand daggers slice into her. 'If I promise to keep that fact firmly in mind, do you think you could still bring yourself to serve up the odd meal or so?'

'Well,' he said, adopting an expression of deep contemplation, 'that depends.'

'On what?'

'On how you conduct yourself today.'

'Maybe I am distantly related to your mother,' she murmured, 'because I've just realised that I'd go to quite staggering lengths to keep you cooking those delicious meals for me.' And to the ends of the earth to keep him here with her like this.

'I sincerely hope we don't have to resort to staggering lengths,' he murmured enigmatically. 'Perhaps we should just start off at a discreet distance,' he added, then turned his attention to finishing off his egg.

'Was I supposed to understand that?' asked Maggie. She helped herself to another slice of toast, laughter dancing in her eyes as she tried to make out what he was up to.

'Just think about it, Maggie,' he replied, flashing her

an infuriating grin as he picked up his coffee-cup and drained it. 'The only way we're going to get through a full day's work is if you keep your distance from me. . . and looking at me like that counts as not keeping your distance.'

'Oh, I see,' she chuckled. 'It's all down to me, is it?'

'Of course it is,' he replied, rising. 'Because I have this gut feeling I'm going to prove to have no will-power at all around you. And I'm sorry to hurry you over what could prove to be your last meal prepared by me, but we're already late setting off.'

Never once during the hours that followed did even his hand so much as brush against Maggie's and nor did Slane make any reference to the night they had shared.

Despite his earlier joking remarks about his probably having no will-power where she was concerned, Maggie at first felt slightly put out at his apparent lack of temptation to put it to the test.

Later her thoughts took a bleaker turn as she reminded herself that, unlike her, he wasn't in love, which was why he was able to compartmentalise night and day with such ease. By the time they had reached the house that evening, after having stopped off for a meal on the way back, as they had worked much later than usual, she had convinced herself that he was no longer physically interested in her.

'Trust a batch as tricky as that one to turn up on us today of all days,' groaned Slane as they let themselves into the house. 'But I'm very proud of you,' he added softly, turning towards her as he shrugged off his coat.

'I don't see why,' she muttered, the longings which pounded through her making it impossible for her to raise her eyes to his as she too removed her coat. 'I'd rather get a batch like that finished in one go than have to face it again in the morning.'

'That wasn't what I meant,' he said, taking her coat from her and hanging it up with his. 'And tomorrow I'll cook you a meal to die for, OK?'

She raised her eyes to his and the next moment was in his arms.

'I nearly suggested we call it a day at lunchtime,' he groaned indistinctly after his mouth had finished a particularly thorough investigation of hers.

'If you had I'd have told you that was the best idea I'd ever heard,' she breathed ecstatically, clasping her arms around his neck as though she would never let him go.

'Maggie, you mustn't say things like that. What happens tomorrow when I remember what you've said just now?' he groaned, then picked her up and swung her around dizzily. 'I had thought about carrying you up the stairs,' he chuckled as he returned her to her feet. 'But then I decided I'd better conserve my strength.'

'Perhaps I should carry you,' offered Maggie, burying her face against his chest and feeling as though her own would burst.

'No, I can't have you tiring yourself out,' he murmured, releasing her and taking her by the hand. 'If you like you can fill the tub and I'll scrub your back,' he added, pulling her after him as he began racing up the stairs. He halted halfway up. 'Or I could fill the. . .' He hauled her back into his arms. 'Or we could just skip the bath till later.'

And that set the pattern for a large part of the ever decreasing time left to them; days passed in the strangely formal ritual of work, followed by nights filled with mind-blowing passion.

Maggie gave up trying to find an answer to the dichotomy she found inexplicable in their relationship—their diametrically opposed reasons for being involved—and gradually became locked in a time-warp in which only the immediate present existed. . .until a couple of days before it was all due to end and Slane began chipping away at the wall with which she had surrounded herself by introducing the subject of the future.

'You never did get around to telling me what you'll be doing when you get back to London,' he stated out of the blue as they dawdled around a large supermarket, on what, it suddenly hit Maggie, would probably be their last shopping trip together. It was a subject that he had broached earlier and which she, shaken to find just how fragile her defences were against even the slightest invasion of reality, had managed to sidestep. 'Will you be going back to Body and Soul, or what?'

'For a while,' she replied, picking up a bunch of grapes and placing them in the trolley, and wishing with all her heart that he would drop the subject. Getting herself through the next couple of days had become her only priority; the future was a concept that she had blanked from her mind.

'And then what?' he persisted, rummaging through a display of apples and almost demolishing it.

She glanced at him and felt her heart constrict with love. Dressed in jeans and a white sweatshirt beneath an open long dark coat, he pondered over the apples, looking absorbed and impossibly attractive.

'And then what, Maggie?' he repeated, glancing up

and catching her looking at him. He mouthed a loud kiss at her. 'Well?'

'I really don't know,' she replied offhandedly. 'The new people take over just after the new year and they know I won't be staying on because of my teacher training.'

'But you won't start that until next September—Hey, Kieran!' he suddenly called out, depositing the apples in the trolley and striding over to a sockily built, fair-haired man who was contemplating an array of cut flowers with an air of bemusement.

The man's face lit up with a look of delighted incredulity as he caught sight of Slane. 'Talk of the devil,' he roared as the two exchanged a brief hug. 'I've been trying to track you down for days now. There doesn't seem to be anybody at Connor's place, so we've been ringing around the hotels—'

'But I haven't let anyone know I'm back,' laughed Slane. 'So how—?'

'No, you haven't, you devil. And why not?'

'Because this trip is strictly business and I couldn't afford to be led astray by the likes of you,' declared Slane. 'Hell, it's good to see you, though. . .'

Maggie watched as the two became engrossed in conversation, the thought occurring to her that all his evenings had been free and had it not been for her he perhaps would have contacted his old Dublin friends. She had almost decided that she might as well get on with the little shopping they needed when Slane, miming abject apologies, returned to her side with the other man in tow.

'Sorry to have abandoned you like that,' he said, 'but I'm practically in shock from running into this guy. Maggie, meet Kieran McBride, an old Dublin school buddy of mine. Kieran, this is Maggie Wallace, a protégée of Connor's who's helping me out with that project I was telling you about.'

As Maggie shook hands with the smiling Irishman her mind was turning over his description of her as Connor's protégée and resenting it. But then, she supposed resignedly, he was hardly likely to introduce her as the woman with whom he spent exhausting nights.

'It's grand meeting you, Maggie,' said Kieran, turning back to Slane and shaking his head. 'Look, Fiona—my wife—and I are off out this evening. I only dropped in here to get some flowers on the way back from fetching the babysitter. I can't believe you're off again on Saturday,' he groaned. 'Can the pair of you make it for dinner tomorrow evening?'

Slane glanced at Maggie, then nodded.

'Fine—I'll ring you first thing in the morning and let you know how to get to my place,' he called out to them, racing over to the flowers and picking up the first bunch that came to hand. 'I'll have to run!'

'Hey, Kieran, you didn't say how you knew I was here,' Slane's laughing voice called after him as he dashed to the checkout.

'It's a story and half, so I'll tell you all about it tomorrow!'

'Kieran was always one of Marjorie's favourites,' reminisced Slane as they resumed their shopping. 'Perhaps I should have contacted him and a couple of the others, but we all have so much to catch up on, I thought it better to leave it till I was back here on vacation... Still, it was good seeing him again.'

'Why don't you visit him on your own tomorrow?'

suggested Maggie as they queued up at the checkout. 'Then you can do all the catching up you want.'

'We will do anyway,' he chuckled, 'so you and his wife will have to entertain one another— His wife!' he exclaimed suddenly, then shook his head in disbelief. 'I mean, I knew he was married—I was invited to the wedding but couldn't make it—but it hadn't really sunk in. Yet from what he said about a babysitter it seems he's also a father!'

'How absolutely amazing,' murmured Maggie drily, 'and he a mere child in his thirties—or has all the responsibility made him look older than he actually is?'

'My, you're very catty all of a sudden,' he commented, loading the contents of the trolley onto the conveyor belt. 'Kieran and I were around nine years old when we first met and his only love was rugby— you know, the football game with the—'

'Slane, I do know what rugby is,' Maggie cut in, smiling at the young checkout girl who had grinned involuntarily at what she was hearing. 'It's American football that I can make neither head nor tail of.'

'I'll tell you all there is to know about it later,' he murmured, and flashed the young girl a dazzling smile. 'Or would you rather I explained it all now—to the pair of you?' he asked the now giggling girl.

'I beg of you,' groaned Maggie, 'please don't.' And she put their purchases in a bag as he paid for them.

'Be sure and come back and tell me why they all wear spacesuits to play in,' the girl whispered to Maggie, and dissolved into laughter when Slane indignantly threatened to call the manager.

'She's right,' mused Maggie as they got into the car. 'Why do American foot—?'

'Are you planning on doing the cooking tonight?' he interrupted threateningly.

'You're so much better at it than I am,' grovelled Maggie unashamedly.

'So what was that you were about to ask about American footballers?' he enquired, driving off.

'My mind's suddenly gone completely blank.'

'Well, mine hasn't—we were talking about Kieran. All I was going to say was that the last real time I spent with him he had just started medical school and was still more interested in rugby even then than he was in women... Hell, why am I subjecting myself to this tortuous explanation?'

'Why indeed?' murmured Maggie.

'That wasn't by any chance Miss Prim taking over, was it?' he asked uneasily.

'Of course it wasn't!' she exclaimed indignantly.

'Glad to hear it,' he replied, catching her hand and raising it briefly to his lips. 'Has she gone for good?'

'Yes, she's gone for good,' replied Maggie, so completely thrown by his spontaneous affectionate gesture that it took all of her minimal acting powers to keep her words reasonably light. 'I wonder how your friend Kieran knew you were here?' she continued, desperate to change the subject.

'So do I... Maggie, you didn't mind my saying we'd go round there tomorrow, did you?'

'Of course I didn't!' she exclaimed, surprised. 'What makes you ask?'

'You just seemed a little out of sorts,' he said, flashing her a sideways glance. 'On second thoughts, though, it started before we ran into Kieran. Why are you so reluctant to discuss what you plan doing between now and starting your teacher training course?'

'I'm not reluctant to discuss it!' she exclaimed exasperatedly, her heart sinking. 'It's just that I've no idea what plans the new people have for replacing me—I've told them I'll stay on until they find someone, but for all I know I could be out of work the day after they arrive.'

'And that worries you?' he asked as they drew up in front of the house.

'Well, I suppose it won't be that easy finding a job until I go back to college,' she admitted. She pulled a face as she got out of the car. 'Actually, it would be much easier if I could stay on at Body and Soul for a few months—because of my mother and Jim.'

'What—you're helping them financially?' he asked, aghast, as they entered the house.

Maggie shook her head, laughing. 'Oh, no—in fact one of the problems I had about Jim in the bad old days was that he's pretty well off. Not mega-rich like the Fitzpatricks, but—'

'Sorry to interrupt,' he murmured, reaching out and pulling her to him, 'but this filthy-rich capitalist needs a quick fix,' he added, and kissed her soundly. 'You were saying?' He grinned, releasing her and removing his coat.

'I. . . I've lost my train of thought,' she croaked, the knowledge—which she could no longer avoid—of how little time she had left with him pounding destructively through her. 'Oh, yes—Jim's money. It's not even as though he flashes it around or anything, but he is very generous. . .and I bitterly resented that at first.

'You see, on Dad's salary, even though my mother and I never went without anything, we always had to save for things like holidays and special treats. When I was at university I would scrub floors rather than let Jim help me out when I was broke—which was usually all the time.'

'I guess I can understand that,' chuckled Slane as they took the shopping to the kitchen. 'But what's that got to do with your leaving Body and Soul?'

'I've a nasty feeling that the moment I leave there the pair of them have plans to whisk me off to their place and spoil me.'

'And that's a bad thing?' he enquired, inspecting the steaks he was unwrapping.

Maggie, who had just tipped some new potatoes into a colander and was about to take them to the sink, looked over at him, startled by the note of censure that had entered his voice. She might love him to distraction, she told herself bemusedly, but she often hadn't the slightest idea how his mind was working.

'Perhaps not,' she muttered defensively, taking the potatoes to the sink and scrubbing at them with unwarranted vigour. 'But I'm not a child and have no wish to be treated like one.'

'No, you're not a child,' he agreed, 'but I dare say your mother and stepfather are fully aware of that fact.'

'And what's that supposed to mean?' she demanded hotly, the peculiarly negative feelings that had been building up in her erupting suddenly into aggression.

'Are you through with those potatoes yet?' he asked, ignoring her question.

Maggie tipped the scrubbed potatoes into a saucepan and added some water. She took the pan to the cooker. 'I didn't mean to snap,' she sighed as she turned on the heat. 'Would you like me to make some coffee while those are doing?'

'No—I'll have wine,' he replied, giving her an unnervingly thoughtful look as he reached for the corkscrew. 'Would you like some?'

She nodded, busying herself getting glasses and wondering why she didn't just do what every nerve in her body ached to do—simply walk up to him, put her arms around him and rest her head against him. It was all crazy, she told herself miserably; if she hadn't loved him she wouldn't have hesitated to put her arms around him, whereas he, uninhibited by any such emotion, could reach out to her with complete spontaneity.

He poured them both a glass of wine. 'It needs to breathe a while,' he muttered after taking a sip.

'Would you like me to do anything with the courgettes?' asked Maggie, feeling slightly snubbed by his lack of response to her apology.

He looked at her blankly.

'The courgettes,' she said, waving one of them in front of him.

'I wondered what on earth you were talking about.' He grinned. 'We call them zucchini. No, leave them, thanks; they won't take me a minute to do.' He walked over to her and put his arms around her, resting his chin on her head and rocking her gently.

'What is it about you?' he sighed softly. 'When I'm cooking you a meal you always seem to feel you have to run around helping. And what's wrong with your mother and Jim pampering you for a while?'

'Nothing; I. . . I don't know what's got into me,' she whispered, burying her face against him. 'Just ignore me.'

'Your trouble is that you're half dead on your feet,'

he said, stroking her hair. 'Perhaps we should sort out our sleeping arrangements tonight to ensure we don't start off tomorrow like a couple of zombies.'

This time she couldn't stop herself acting spontaneously—she shook her head vigorously.

'Perhaps you're right,' he chuckled. 'In a couple of days from now we'll have all the time in the world to catch up on lost sleep.' He eased her away from him and planted a kiss on her forehead. 'Meanwhile I have a meal to see to.'

Maggie sat down at the table, clutching her wine glass as she accepted what had been creeping up on her for some time now—the realisation that the nearer it got to the time they would part, the less she would be able to cope.

Of course she had known that she would be devastated when the time came, which was no doubt why she had so ruthlessly closed her mind even to contemplating it... But somehow she had managed to convince herself that the devastation would come once they had parted, not start threatening her now, when she was in no fit state to cope with it.

'How do you like your steak?' he asked.

'Pink, not bloody, thank you,' she replied, rising, then hesitating. 'Am I allowed to lay the table?'

'Well...perhaps as a special treat,' he conceded. 'You can also drain those potatoes and throw a knob of butter on them too, if you like.'

The more she strove to sound bright and cheery during the meal, the more inscrutable became the looks he gave her, and the closer she knew she was to becoming overwhelmed by feelings of utter hopelessness.

And later, when he held her passively to him for a

long time before making love to her, she accepted that the hunger in him had aleady begun to wane, as she knew it inevitably must without love to sustain it, and she felt a glimmer of hope that, if nothing else, her pride would keep her together for the time they had left, which could now be counted in hours.

CHAPTER NINE

'FIONA, that was a magnificent meal,' declared Slane, smiling across the dinner-table at his friend's vivacious, dark-haired wife. 'And if that devil of a husband of yours hadn't already snapped you up I'd be beating a path to your door.'

'It really was wonderful, Fiona,' agreed Maggie, who after a day of feeling as though she had been teetering on the edge of a precipice since the moment she had awoken, had slowly begun to unwind in the welcoming, easygoing company of the McBrides.

'Thank you both, but I'll be honest with you,' laughed Fiona. 'Of all the million and one things Kieran had told me about Slane, the only thing I could remember, when he said he'd invited you round for a meal, was that Slane was such a great cook... So, the next time we all eat a meal together, Slane, you can cook it!'

'Done,' he chuckled, 'though you might have to wait a while for it—but not too long, I hope.'

'Does that mean you're planning on letting us know next time?' enquired Kieran wryly. 'Because—'

'That reminds me,' leapt in Slane. 'How *did* you know I was here?'

'From a road-accident victim,' murmured Kieran innocently.

'A what?' exlaimed Slane.

'Just stop it, Kieran,' groaned his wife, smiling

reassuringly at Slane. 'My cousin Michael is with a pop group that's hit the jackpot and—'

'Hattie Lang!' groaned Slane.

'That's right,' laughed Fiona. 'Poor Hattie was involved in a car crash on her way to the airport. She had a bit of a bang on the head, but flatly refused to be taken to a hospital—so Michael rang Kieran to be on the safe side.'

'Was she OK?' asked Slane.

'Just a mild concussion,' said Kieran. 'We kept her here for the night and she caught a plane the next day. But somewhere along the line your name came up, and I was beginning to wonder if I hadn't misdiagnosed her when she said she'd run into you here.'

'You're almost beginning to make me feel bad,' chuckled Slane, then he grew serious. 'But being here with you now makes me realise I've left it far too long coming back.'

'Mind you, it must have been tough knowing Marjorie wouldn't be here to make sure you wiped your feet and wrapped up warm,' sighed Kieran. 'That must have been the last time you were over—when we all said our goodbyes to her.'

'It was,' said Slane. 'Though, as you both know, I did try moving heaven and earth to get to your wedding— but they just wouldn't shift.'

'But that wedding telegram of yours just about made up for it,' laughed Kieran. 'Aiden Kelly was my best man and he read out every slanderous word of it... Fiona's mother took a lot of very careful handling to recover from it!'

'My God I'd almost forgotten about that wretched telegram!' exclaimed Fiona. 'Kieran, what did you do with that carving-knife? I need it!'

'How about if we clear up and make the coffee?' offered Slane, grinning. 'Would that help make up for it?'

'You'd need to wipe down the walls and scrub the floor as well,' chuckled Fiona, 'and then... Oh, no!' she groaned as the sound of a child's crying suddenly filled the room. 'It seems our son and heir has decided he's missing out on all the fun.' She got to her feet, went over to the intercom and turned it down. 'So, you men off to your chores in the kitchen while Maggie and I see to junior.'

Maggie rose and followed her from the dining room.

'They'll probably take for ever in there,' Fiona smiled. 'But at least we'll be spared another couple of hours of listening to their reminiscences. If you want to go in and stretch out in front of the fire while I see to Colm you go ahead.'

'I'd love to see him,' said Maggie. 'But perhaps seeing a stranger would upset him?'

'Upset him?' laughed Fiona, motioning her to follow her up the stairs. 'He'll be over the moon once he's given you a careful inspection.'

Colm McBride had his father's fair hair and his mother's dark eyes and greeted them both with boisterous delight.

'He's gorgeous,' sighed Maggie, who had always got on very well with the few babies she had met. 'How old is he?'

'It was his first birthday last week,' replied Fiona. 'Colm, this is Maggie—she's from England.'

Maggie reached out a finger, which was treated to a solemn-eyed inspection but not accepted.

'He doesn't usually wake at night,' said Fiona, laying him down on the changing-table, 'but when he does a change of nappy and a warm drink soon get him off again. Though I suppose it wouldn't hurt this once for him to come downstairs and meet his gorgeous uncle Slane.'

She flashed Maggie a mischievous look. 'OK, so you've made it plain it's nothing but a chance business relationship—but my God, Maggie, how does a normal woman keep her hands off a hunk like that while working in a confined space with him day after day?'

'When you're doing the mind-bogglingly boring sort of work we've been involved in,' replied Maggie, actually managing a smile, 'pretty easily.'

'Obviously you already have someone special in your life, otherwise you wouldn't be talking like that,' laughed Fiona. 'Were you with Slane when he ran into Hattie?'

Maggie nodded, grateful that the subject had been changed. 'I rather liked what little I saw of her—she seemed quite a character.'

'She was a gas. She never stopped talking the whole time she was here—and what talk! It seems she used to be a gossip columnist but now she's gone up-market. You'd never believe some of the things she told me— just name a name and she'd come up with something juicy. And some of the things she claims that that dish down in my kitchen has been up to. . .'

She rolled her eyes theatrically. 'Though, according to her, no less than Felicity Field, the actress, has him as good as hooked. God, can you imagine it—Kieran coming back from the hospital one evening and saying, By the way, Slane's coming round to dinner and he's bringing Felicity Field?'

Laughing, she bent down and rubbed her nose against the gurgling baby's stomach. 'And that's just the sort of thing that dada of yours is capable of doing to your poor mama, isn't it, precious?' She picked up the baby, who immediately stretched out his arms to Maggie.

Maggie took him, grateful to have the warm, solid bundle of his small body to concentrate on, instead of the cold desolation with which Fiona's laughing words had filled her.

'Now you be a good boy and try not to drool all over Maggie's lovely dress,' warned his mother as they descended the stairs, with Maggie clutching the baby to her with one hand and clinging to the banister with the other, terrified that she would trip.

'Listen to those two, would you?' exclaimed Fiona as sounds of male laughter reached them. 'Now, come and meet your uncle Slane,' she said to the baby as she and Maggie entered the kitchen.

'You're not going to make the poor child call me Uncle, are you?' groaned Slane after Fiona had formally introduced them, reaching out a finger and tentatively stroking the small head wedged against Maggie's shoulder.

'Well, I've only the one brother and Kieran hasn't any,' laughed Fiona, 'so he's a bit short on uncles.'

'And stop prodding the poor child,' teased Kieran. 'Take him and have a good look at him—that's what you and some poor unfortunate woman will be producing one of these days... And for God's sake don't drop him!' he added on a sudden note of panic as Slane clumsily took the baby from Maggie.

'I'll bet your dad's dropped you a few times,' Slane informed Colm, holding him awkwardly aloft, 'unless he's improved since the days I was forced to practise passing rugby balls to him.'

'That's right, son,' chuckled Kieran as the baby gazed balefully at Slane. 'You give him the evil eye.'

'Kieran, isn't that the phone?' exclaimed Fiona from the cooker where she was heating a drink for Colm.

'Watch him with that son of mine,' Kieran ordered Maggie as he left the room.

The baby swivelled round to see his departing father, then saw Maggie. He glanced back at the man holding him, then turned and raised his arms to Maggie with an almost pleading smile.

'I can't say I blame you,' murmured Slane to the child as he passed him back to Maggie. 'When do they start walking and talking?' he asked Fiona.

'He's already doing a bit of both,' she replied, rinsing out a bottle. She glanced over at Maggie, against whom her son was snuggled in cherubic silence. 'My, you have made a hit there, Maggie—I do believe he's dropped off.'

Slane bent down to examine the silent bundle. 'Hell, do they all fall asleep that fast?' he exclaimed. He glanced at Maggie, his oddly cool expression tinged with mockery. 'He suits you. You should think about getting one of your own.'

'Slane!' exclaimed Fiona indignantly. 'You're talking as though babies were a fashion accessory, for heaven's sake! I think it's time this wee lad was back in his cot,' she said, walking over to them and taking her sleeping son from Maggie. 'And we can forget about that bottle I've just made up—he's dead to the world. You go on into the living room, Maggie,' she added as her husband returned, 'and let these two get on with their chores.'

Maggie did as she was told and sat down in a large armchair next to the fire. She leaned her head back and watched the flickering flames through half-closed eyes.

Holding the baby in her arms had stirred feelings in her that she had never before experienced. . .but then the past two weeks had been one endless stream of feelings she had never before experienced. Disturbed by the effect the baby was still having on her, she forced her mind back over the day.

Apart from this evening it had been a day she would gladly have erased from her life. On the surface it had been little different from any of their others, but beneath the surface she had detected all the signs that Slane wanted it finished and behind him every bit as much as she now did, though for reasons which were the antithesis of hers.

She put her hands to her temples and pressed against them as the thought occurred to her that, with his ardour cooling as rapidly as it appeared to be, at least she wasn't likely to find herself in the humiliating position of declaring her undying love for him in the few, rapidly diminishing hours left to them.

She gave a sharp cry of fright as her hands were replaced by cool fingers stroking lightly at her temples.

'Sorry, I didn't mean to startle you,' said Slane, straightening and walking round to the side of the chair. 'Have you got a headache?'

'No, I. . . It was so cosy in here, I—I nearly dozed off,' she stammered.

'It's been a long day,' he said, his eyes curiously expressionless as he squatted beside her chair and looked up at her. 'We can go after we've had coffee; Kieran's just bringing it in.'

'And here he is on cue,' came the Irishman's jovial

voice as he strode in and placed a tray on the coffee-table. 'Now—who's going to be mother?'

'Anyone, as long as it's not you,' answered his wife, appearing behind him. She grinned over at Maggie. 'For a neurosurgeon renowned for his steady hand in the operating theatre, he does a lousy job wielding a tea or coffee pot around the home—as the state of my poor carpets will quickly confirm.'

'Do you see how downtrodden I am, Slane?' sighed Kieran as Fiona ruffled his hair and began pouring the coffee.

'Yeah, my heart bleeds for you,' laughed Slane, going over and taking a seat on the sofa next to him.

'And there I was, just about to try to persuade you to stay on at least for a day or two now that you've finished cutting up plants,' complained Kieran. 'Slane, is there really no way you can?'

Slane shook his head. 'I'd love to be able to say yes, but I'll be practically stepping off the flight back and onto one for Tokyo.'

'So, what about this wonder plant of Maurice's—is there any chance of it living up to expectations?'

Slane shrugged. 'I honestly couldn't say. Even if Maurice has managed to replicate it, it could take God only knows how long to find out if it actually has any potential.'

'Well, it's something the medical world could certainly do with,' murmured Kieran. 'And, if it does hold up, all I can say is thank God it's you who'd be patenting it, instead of one of the greedy pharmaceutical companies. Though I dare say testing and marketing something like that would cost a fortune anyway.'

As she remembered her bitter disappointment when Slane had spoken of the fortune to be made from such a drug, Maggie's eyes flew to his, and met with a look of mocking reproach.

'It could do,' he murmured, his gaze switching back to Kieran, 'but we don't even know if we have a viable plant yet. And, having just spent the past two weeks up to my eyeballs in them, you'll probably understand that right now they're not my favourite topic.'

'I can see it isn't with either of you,' chuckled Kieran. 'I think Maggie's about to drop off.'

'I haven't quite,' she laughed, 'but I could easily in front of this fire—it's lovely.'

'But it's time we made a move, anyway,' said Slane, returning his coffee-cup to the table. 'But if you're free tomorrow at around three perhaps you could drop me off at the airport?'

'Of course we will,' said Kieran, rising. 'And will you be leaving at the same time, Maggie?'

She had to struggle to clear her head. 'I. . . N-no, my plane leaves in the morning,' she stammered.

Both Fiona and Kieran hugged her warmly as they said their goodbyes. 'Be sure and look us up any time you're back in Dublin,' urged Fiona. 'And have a safe journey home.'

'They're such an incredibly warm and welcoming couple,' sighed Maggie once they were on their way.

'I have to admit they're a pretty good advertisement for marriage,' murmured Slane, then added abruptly, 'What time is your flight in the morning?'

'I can't remember,' she muttered, turning to gaze sightlessly out of the window. 'I'll have to check.'

Except that there was nothing to check, she thought listlessly, wondering why she had automatically lied instead of admitting that her ticket was an open one and that, until Kieran had brought up the subject, the need to book herself onto a flight had gone clean out of her head.

'Do you think there's any chance of your seeing Connor before he comes back?' she asked, beginning to feel unnerved by the silence developing between them.

'It depends on how quickly I can get back from Japan,' he replied, 'but I doubt it.'

For a while Maggie racked her brains for something else to say, then gave up. He wasn't making any effort, she reminded herself with growing bitterness, so why should she?

For all she knew he might, at the time, have actually believed his pious claims to wanting to free her libido, though she seriously doubted it. What it really boiled down to was that he had seen an opportunity for a brief fling with a woman with whom he had once had a one-night stand and had taken that opportunity, safe in the knowledge that once it was over there would be an entire ocean between him and the possibility of any ensuing little embarrassments. . .

The only inconvenience had been that his interest had flagged before the allotted time had run out.

She would plead tiredness and go straight to her bed, she had decided by the time they arrived back at the house. But not to save him the embarrassment of having to come up with an excuse, she informed herself grimly, but because her pride would have it no other way.

She flinched when he caught her by the arm as they entered the house.

'Maggie, you should know me well enough by now to know that I'd never force myself on you,' he said quietly, his hand dropping from her. 'But please don't revert to giving me the Miss Prim routine.'

'Don't worry, Slane,' she said, unable to keep the bitterness from her voice. 'Your cure has worked— Miss Prim as gone for good.'

'So how come you don't seem too happy about it?'

'I *am* happy.' She sighed unconvincingly. 'It's just that. . . I don't know. . . I—'

'Now that you're cured it's time to stop taking the medicine?'

'I'd hardly put it like that!' she exclaimed, startled not only by his words but also by the bitterness of their tone.

'Well, however you'd put it, I think it's time we celebrated your cure,' he said, removing his coat and flinging it over the banister. 'And I have just the thing. . . You go along to the drawing room and I'll join you in a moment.'

Maggie removed her own coat, then retrieved his and hung them both on the hall stand. So much for her going straight to her room, she thought wearily as she made her way to the drawing room. She went over to the large Georgian windows and drew their curtains.

And so much too for her harsh judgement of him, she told herself as she turned on the table lamps. Yes, his physical need for her probably was on the wane, but even if nine out of ten times she found it impossible to guess what was going on in his mind she honestly didn't believe that he was capable of deliberate cruelty. His coming here had been an ordeal for him and it was little wonder that he was looking forward to putting it behind him.

'Here we are,' he announced, holding aloft a bottle of champagne and two glasses.

'My, we are celebrating!' exclaimed Maggie, making a concerted effort to muster some enthusiasm and taking a seat on the sofa.

He opened the bottle and poured two glasses, passing her one. 'Well, here's to Maggie and the very lucky guy she'll one day find,' he murmured.

Maggie took a sip from her glass, noting wryly that she had already found that man and wondering how he would feel if he knew that. . . Certainly not lucky, she decided.

'And here's to Slane having made it back to Ireland,' she said quietly. 'It must be quite a relief that it's now almost over.'

'What makes you say that?' he asked, sitting down beside her.

'I just meant that this whole trip must have been quite an ordeal for you,' she said, wishing that she had sat on one of the armchairs instead of here where he had joined her.

'This *whole* trip?' he enquired softly.

'Y-you know what I mean,' she stammered, and drained her glass.

'Stop drinking that stuff as though it were lemonade,' he chided, removing the glass from her and refilling it. 'And perhaps I know what you mean this time—' he sighed as he handed her back the glass '—but most of the time I can't seem to figure out what you mean at all.'

'Join the club,' muttered Maggie, then took another swig from her glass.

'What—you can't figure out what you mean either?'

She gave him a startled look, then smiled. 'That's not what I meant. . .but, come to think of it, as I frequently seem to have difficulty working out what's going on in my own mind it's little wonder I have no idea what's going on in yours.'

She regretted the words the instant they were out, convinced that only the most cursory examination of them would reveal clues as to her true feelings for him. 'Look, it's late,' she muttered, placing her glass on the table and leaping to her feet.

'Maggie, I'm a fairly civilised guy,' he said impatiently, rising also. 'I can take a hint, so there's no need for you to—'

'What do you mean, you can take a hint?' she demanded.

'Maggie, if you don't want to spend tonight with me, that's OK. You don't have to—'

'Slane, there really isn't any need for this pretence,' sighed Maggie, angry with him for the clumsiness with which he had tried to preserve her pride but loving him all the same for trying. 'We both knew this would all end tomorrow. . . The fact that you would rather it ended a little earlier is neither here nor there.'

'My God, you really *don't* have any idea what's going on in my mind!' he exclaimed hoarsely.

He reached out for her and pulled her to him. 'If you want me to stop, all you have to do is say so and I will,' he whispered, his hands sliding down her body till they rested against the soft swell of her buttocks. Then he drew her to him, his hands pressing her already awakening body against the rampant arousal of his and instantly demolishing any ideas she had had about him no longer wanting her.

Uttering a ragged, groaning sigh, Maggie flung her arms around his neck and clung to him. 'I just thought. . .' she protested, her words muffled against him. 'I don't know what. . .but I just thought it.'

'And I've just proved you wrong,' he chided huskily. 'But I just thought too, and OK, so you're choking me half to death, but what does that prove? After all, I was subjected to the Miss Prim treatment just a while ago, so maybe you just feel like choking me to death.'

'How can you say that?' she exclaimed. 'I didn't want to hear you making excuses and —'

'You were the one making the excuses,' he teased, 'and I'm the one still waiting to be convinced.'

'Slane, I—' With a groan of exasperation she drew his head down to hers and kissed him. 'Convinced?' she demanded breathlessly.

'Can't really say I am,' he sighed while he slowly unbuttoned her dress.

She kissed him again, this time undoing the buttons of his shirt as she did so. 'Now are you convinced?'

He shook his head. 'I might have been if you'd simply ripped the shirt off my back. I guess you'll just have to try again,' he laughed, starting on her bra as she obligingly stepped out of her dress.

'Though, on the other hand, these little beacons standing so beautifully to attention go a long way towards reassuring me,' he chuckled, hauling her down onto the sofa with him and burying his face against her tautly aroused breasts. 'A long way, but not all the way,' he murmured indistinctly, then brought a sharp, shivering cry of longing from her as he opened his mouth against her and began torturing her flesh with his teeth and tongue.

'How can you dare call me Miss Prim?' she demanded distractedly.

'Easily,' he growled. 'Especially when I've got you stripped down virtually to your pants and all you've managed to do is undo the buttons of my shirt.'

Getting his shirt off him proved to be a major operation, partly because his busily exploring hands refused to co-operate and partly because he was so ticklish. He was far more co-operative over his trousers, obligingly kicking off his shoes before it had occurred to her to suggest that he do so. But once they were off she eased her away from him.

'Stand up,' he whispered, laughing as she tried to throw herself back against him. 'Stand up.'

'Why?'

'Stand up and I'll show you.'

Dazedly she rose to her feet and stood before him. He reached out his hands and placed them on her hips, then slowly began rolling her tights down her body. She reached out and sank her fingers in his hair, and felt the ghosts of all the bleak tomorrows ahead of her shiver through her as the totality of her love for him washed over her.

When she'd stepped out of her tights he wrapped his arms around her and pressed his face against her stomach. Then he raised his head and gazed up at her with dark, unreadable eyes.

'I'm having thoughts I shouldn't be having,' he whispered unsteadily.

'Such as?' she asked equally unsteadily, her heart feeling as though it had stopped.

'I... Maggie, are you certain you won't start having regrets once you're back home?'

It was what she had subconsciously secretly dreaded—the direct question. Awkwardly she placed her arms around him, blocking his view of the tears that had welled in her eyes.

'Regrets?' she asked with just the right amount of

scorn. 'Mr Right isn't going to know what's hit him once I've decided on him.'

'Attagirl,' he muttered, his words muffled against her. 'But, meanwhile, you're not back home yet—so grab that champagne bottle and get yourself up those stairs.'

The last time she awoke, her body battered and bruised from the fierceness of a night of almost war-like lovemaking, she gazed down in the murky half-light at his sleeping face and knew that the lie she had uttered in the drawing room had been her last. . . If he opened his eyes now, the only words he would hear would be those of love.

She lowered her head and brushed her lips softly against his, the greater part of her, hopeless and helpless, willing him to wake. Then she slipped from the bed and left the room, never once looking back at his sleeping form.

CHAPTER TEN

'HELLO, Maggie my darling, how are you?'

'Connor! I was beginning to think you'd disappeared off the face of the earth!' she exclaimed, disturbed to find her heart pounding fit to burst. 'Where are you ringing from?' she asked, more than a little relieved to find her innate sense of humour surfacing as she tried imagining the elderly professor's reaction to knowing the disconcerting effect he was having on her.

'Dublin,' he replied, his voice disintegrating into a hoarse rasp on the second syllable.

'Prof, you sound ghastly,' she gasped, her only feeling now one of alarm.

'This is me well on the road to recovery,' he informed her croakily. 'I haven't had a voice for the past ten days—some damned bug I must have picked up on the flight back.

'Anyway, now that I can actually speak I thought I'd better get in touch with you. I'd hoped to be there to help you celebrate your birthday tomorrow, but, as I'll not be over until next week now, we'll have to have a wee celebration then. So tell me what you have planned for the big day.'

'It's my twenty-fourth, not my fourteenth birthday,' protested Maggie, the idea of being required to celebrate anything, let alone her birthday, filling her with dread. 'Mum and Jim are taking me out for a meal at the weekend. But about you, Prof—you make sure

you're really over whatever it is you've picked up
before you start traipsing back here.'

'God, you're beginning to sound like Mrs Morrison,'
complained the professor. 'She's been carrying on like
some damned Florence Nightingale—'

'Connor, you're almost losing your voice again!' she
exclaimed anxiously. 'We'll speak when you're over.'

'Yes, the old voice is beginning to play up a bit
again,' he croaked, 'but before you hang up I've a
message for you from young Slane.'

Maggie felt suddenly physically ill as the wall which
she had so carefully erected around her feelings by day
began tumbling. 'Oh, yes?'

'Well, not exactly from him—nobody's seen hide nor
hair of him since he handed in the lab breakdown and
took off for Japan, so he probably doesn't even know
yet.'

'Know what?' she asked, her mouth painfully dry.

'The computer results of those analyses the pair of
you did. . . The bad news is that Maurice didn't manage
to come up with a true replica, but the good news is
that he came pretty damned near to doing so with two
or three of the growths, so it's certainly worth him
having another go. I hope you're not too disappointed,
pet.'

'It would have been wonderful if it had come off first
time,' sighed Maggie, drowning in a deluge of
memories.

'Well, Maurice is a man who loves nothing better
than a challenge,' said Connor, 'so I'm sure he'll crack
it yet. How do you think Slane will take the news?' he
asked in an uncharacteristically tentative tone.

'I'm sure no worse than I have,' she replied, having
to force conviction into her tone. 'Now, don't you dare

utter so much as another word—we'll talk all you like next week.'

She put the phone down, then folded her arms on her desk and rested her head on them.

In Ireland she had kept herself going with thoughts of being able to relax and lick her wounds once she had returned to England—but things hadn't turned out as simply as that. She had gone straight to her mother and Jim's on arriving back, but had ended up having to act her heart out to maintain an appearance of normality.

From then on her life had become an impossible see-saw—daytimes during which her every feeling was switched off followed by nights of endless torment. By separating day from night she had convinced herself that she was coping. . .until the moment she had heard Connor's voice and day had become night.

'Maggie—what's wrong, love?'

She jumped at the sound of Helen Morgan's voice; Helen was the company's accountant and friend of Marjorie Fitzpatrick who had been with Body and Soul since its inception.

'Nothing, I—' She broke off, horrified to discover just how close she was to tears. 'It's just that I had a rotten night last night. I'm afraid you caught me almost dozing off!'

'Maggie, you haven't been your usual self ever since you got back from Ireland,' said Helen gently. 'Look, I know you've always said you're quite happy to leave once Mrs Cook and her daughter take over but they're the nicest people you could possibly meet and, if you're worried about what you'll do till you return to unversity I'm sure they'd be only too—'

'No, it's not that at all!' exclaimed Maggie, more

than a little disturbed to discover that she hadn't been coping nearly as well as she had been kidding herself she had. 'In fact, I saw them both the day after I got back and they offered to let me stay on until the summer. And you're right—they really are two of the nicest people you could meet.'

'So why haven't you taken them up on their offer?' asked Helen, her tone openly anxious.

'I. . . Because I've already one or two things lined up,' lied Maggie awkwardly, the truth being that she had had the crazy idea that the sooner she was able to cut herself off from her old, familiar surroundings, the sooner she would be able to start putting her life back together again.

'Well, one thing's for sure,' sighed Helen, eyeing her concernedly, 'we've got to do something about those nasty black circles round your eyes. So you get yourself home and into your bed—and even if it takes till Christmas I don't want to see you again until they're gone. That sleepless night of yours was probably an overdue warning, because, my dear, you really haven't been looking at all well for quite some time.'

'Perhaps you're right,' said Maggie, guilt niggling at her as she gazed sightlessly down at her desktop. She hated deceiving someone as kindly as Helen. 'I haven't been feeling too good for the past few days.' And she would collapse if she didn't get some sleep, she thought with a stab of alarm, realising that in the entire period she had been back she had probably had less sleep than would have constituted one reasonable night's worth.

'Well, off you go,' said Helen, placing an arm round her shoulders and giving them an affectionate squeeze. 'And, just to make sure you do, I'll be back in a while to check that you're not here.'

Maggie cleared her desk, then leaned against it, her legs feeling wobbly beneath her. One thing was for sure, she told herself exasperatedly—if she didn't get her act together pretty soon she'd end up a physical wreck. She was just about to get her things when the phone rang.

'Maggie, it's Rose. You couldn't be a love and watch the shop for me for about ten minutes, could you? I forgot a prescription I had to pick up from my doctor.'

'I'll be right down,' promised Maggie.

She collected her coat and bag and went down to the shop. The instant she entered it she was assailed by memories of her very first impressions of Body and Soul—the exotic yet warmly welcoming mixture of scents that hung delicately in the air, contrasting so pleasingly with the pristine, almost austere lines of its design.

'You're a treasure, Maggie!' exclaimed Rose as she dashed to the door. 'I promise not to be long. Ignore those aromatherapy phials—I'll finish stacking them when I get back.'

Glad of something to do, Maggie took the carton of phials to the shelves and began sorting and stacking them into their allotted places. No sooner had she got into the swing of what she was doing than the gentle tinkle of wind chimes warned her that someone had entered the shop.

For the briefest of moments the thought skittered through her head that she was hallucinating, then she reached out and clutched the shelf nearest her for sorely needed support as Slane strode into the shop.

'My, this is some welcome,' he drawled, shoving his hands deep into the pockets of his coat.

'S-Slane, you're the last person I expected to walk

through that door,' she stammered, frantically willing her wits to restore themselves. 'What on earth are you doing here?'

'I was around—so I thought I'd drop in and see you.'

'Oh. . .well, that was very nice of you, but as you can see I'm rather busy.'

'I don't see a full shop,' he said, pointedly looking around him. 'But no problem—I can wait till you're free.'

'But I don't finish till five,' she protested, almost staggering across the floor to the safety of the counter. 'And I'm—' She broke off, remembering Connor's telephone call. 'Connor rang and told me the results of the test. I know you must be disappointed, but at least—'

'So, they were no good?' he enquired, almost indifferently.

'You mean you don't know?' she asked, completely thrown.

'Would I be asking if I did?' he said shortly, his gaze cool almost to the point of hostility.

Maggie felt the blood rush to her pallid cheeks. Of course he was feeling hostile—she had left Dublin without so much as the scribbled note she would have left had the words not refused to come. She tensed as his shoulders hunched in a sudden gesture of impatience.

'Maurice didn't manage to replicate the plant—but two or three of the growths were promising enough for it to be worth him trying again.'

'Great.'

'So you're not too disappointed?'

'Maggie, I—' He broke off as Rose entered by one door and Helen another.

'Maggie, I thought I ordered you home!' exclaimed Helen with mock severity, then glanced over at Slane and did a double take. 'Good heavens—Slane!' she exclaimed delightedly, rushing over to him.

'Helen.' He beamed, his pleasure undisguised as they hugged warmly.

Maggie watched in dazed silence as the two exchanged animated greetings. Helen had been one of Marjorie's closest friends, she reminded herself, so there was nothing that unusual about her knowing Slane.

'Wow, who's the hunk?' whispered Rose, joining Maggie behind the counter.

'Connor's cousin,' replied Maggie, retrieving her coat and bag and wondering if she could slip out without being noticed.

'Hey, Maggie, where are you off to?' demanded Slane as she sidled towards the door.

'She's going home as she's been told to,' replied Helen for her. 'The state she came back from Ireland in, I'm beginning to wonder if Connor didn't have her out digging roads while she was there.'

'Or digging over his garden, if I know him,' murmured Slane, with a grin, but there was a decidedly guarded look in the eyes meeting Maggie's. He turned back to Helen. 'Leave her to me,' he said. 'I'll see that she gets home to rest—even if I have to tuck her up in her bed myself.'

Ignoring the somewhat startled reaction of both the other women, he walked over to Maggie, took her by the arm and led her to the door.

'I'll give you a call, Helen,' he promised before bustling Maggie outside.

'Slane, I'm perfectly capable of seeing myself home,' protested Maggie, removing her arm from his.

'I was lying.' He grinned. 'I hadn't planned on taking you straight home.' Then his face grew serious as his eyes scanned her face. 'Though I must say Helen has a point—you do look as though you've been out digging roads.'

'Thanks a million,' she retorted, stung by his words. 'You're not looking too great yourself.' And he wasn't, she thought, feeling like screaming with frustration as anxiety stabbed sharply through her. The fact that his eyes were surrounded by dark circles and he looked completely exhausted was no business of hers whatsoever.

'Yeah, well, I have an excuse—what's yours?'

'That I'm probably coming down with a dose of flu,' she replied a trifle defensively. 'Which reminds me— Connor hasn't been at all well since he got back. He's still in Dublin, so perhaps you could go over and see him.'

'I might just do that,' he said. 'I'm staying at his apartment, which is one of the reasons why I came round to see you.'

Maggie gave him a puzzled look then wished she hadn't looked at him at all. It wasn't just that her anixety over his appearance increased tenfold, it was the terrible ache of longing that swept over her that made her wonder just how long she could last before betraying herself.

'Maggie, why did you run off on me like that again?' he demanded hoarsely.

'Slane, there isn't any point in going over all that,' she protested, her voice trembling.

'You still don't know how my minds works, do you?'

he sighed, then shrugged. 'But right now I have this little problem that I believe you can help me solve.'

'What sort of problem?' she asked guardedly, finding her eyes more and more drawn to those handsome, faintly ravaged features.

'I have a set of keys to Connor's apartment, just in case I ever need to use the place when he's not around. But he has this anti-burglar system which I'm hoping you know how to operate, because the idea of the cops landing on the doorstep again—'

'You mean you didn't turn it off and the police arrived?' exclaimed Maggie, astounded to find that she was still actually capable of laughter.

'Yeah, well, I'm glad you find it so funny,' he growled. '*Do* you know how the darned thing works?'

She nodded, still laughing.

'And, when you've finished enjoying yourself so much at my expense, *are* you prepared to come back there with me and show me how it works?'

'I can hardly believe you're telling me you're incapable of—'

'I'm incapable—OK?' he exclaimed impatiently. 'So how about it?'

The instant she nodded his arm went up to hail a passing taxi. Once inside they sat at opposite ends of the seat.

'You promised me Miss Prim had gone for good,' he mocked softly, gazing over at her.

'So I lied,' she snapped, the words out before she could stop them. 'Look, Slane, if you want me to show you how to operate the—'

'OK, OK—no more references to Miss Prim.'

She had expected him to hand her the keys to Connor's flat once they arrived; instead he kept them after using them to let them through the main entrance. When he closed the front door of the flat itself behind them she held out her hand for the keys.

'You have thirty seconds from opening the front door to switching off the. . .' Her words petered to a halt as he marched past her and into the cloakroom containing the alarm panel. 'You knew perfectly well how to operate it!' she exclaimed indignantly as she arrived at the door of the cloakroom just in time to see him finish disarming the alarm.

'I guess I'm not the halfwit you were so ready to believe I was,' he replied, shrugging out of his coat. 'I couldn't think of another way of getting you here.'

'Didn't it occur to you simply to ask?' demanded Maggie.

'Would you have come?'

'I don't know,' she replied unsteadily, and turned towards the front door. 'All I know is that I'm leaving now.' Because there was no guaranteeing that her pride would ever recover from the consequences of her staying a moment longer.

'Maggie, what did I ever do to you to deserve this sort of treatment?' he asked quietly.

'What do you mean?' she gasped, frozen to the spot, not only by his words but by the chilling bleakness of their tone.

'OK, so you don't reckon there's any point in telling me why you took off without a word from Dublin,' he stated woodenly. 'But, whether you like it or not, we were lovers the last time we met. Yet when I walked into the store a while back you acted as though we were barely acquainted. But I guess that answers the question of whether or not you regret what happened between us in Dublin.'

He walked over to her, took her by the shoulders and turned her to face him. 'You regretted it the first time and then the second time,' he told her hoarsely. 'And what about this time—and the next? Because it's always going to be like this for us, Maggie. . .or do you plan on finding someone to cure you of me?'

'The way you claimed you wanted to cure me?' she exploded bitterly.

'Maggie, I wouldn't have expected any woman in her right mind to swallow a line as corny as that,' he stated with startling candour. 'Except that in my case there happened to be— Maggie, no!' he groaned as the dam finally broke in her and she slumped against him, tears coursing silently down her cheeks.

'I've got to go,' she choked through the sobs now racking her. 'It's better if I go. . .'

'Better for who?' he demanded harshly. 'Certainly not for me, and whatever it is you have bottled up inside you like this can't be doing you much good either.' He eased her from him and removed her coat. 'Come on,' he urged in more gentle tones. 'You and I are going to sit down with a good stiff drink each—I reckon we could both use one.'

He led her into the living room and sat her down on the huge-cushioned sofa. He switched on several table lamps before returning to her side, where he knelt before her and slipped off her shoes. 'Now get your feet up while I fix the drinks,' he said, rising. 'Brandy OK for you?'

Maggie drew her legs up beneath her, then buried her head in a cushion as even so simple a response proved beyond her.

'I decided on brandy for you anyway,' he announced,

handing her first a box of tissues then a glass before sitting down next to her.

Maggie dabbed at her face with one of the tissues, then took a sip of the brandy. 'Why couldn't you have left well alone?' she demanded wearily. 'You'll be wishing you had any minute now and it serves you damned well right.'

'You've never understood how my mind works any more than I have yours,' he observed quietly. 'So what makes you think either of us is any judge of what the other might or might not wish?'

Maggie took another sip of her drink, shuddering as its mellow fire trickled slowly down her throat, then shifted her position and hugged her arms around her knees. It was time she got this over and done with, she told herself wearily, closing her eyes as she tried to summon up the courage to speak.

'I didn't *want* you to understand me!' were the words that burst involuntarily from her. 'Everything I let you believe was little more than a pack of lies!' She took a deep breath in an effort to calm herself. 'I would have saved myself an awful lot of. . .of bother if I'd simply swallowed my pride and told you the truth when I first met you in Dublin.' She paused, took another deep breath and told him everything that had preceded their encounter in Brighton.

When she had finished he rose, glass in hand, and without uttering a word went over to one of the tall lattice windows and gazed out onto the street below.

'I tried to tell you in Dublin,' she stated raggedly, devastated by his reaction, 'but my timing wasn't too good.' Just before and again just after they had made love her timing could have more accurately been described as appalling, she reflected bitterly, gazing over at his motionless figure and feeling anger stir within her at the completeness of his rejection.

'Mind you,' she added, bitterness and mounting anger spilling over into her words, 'it would have been interesting to see which would have won out then— lust, or the disgust you're so effortlessly displaying now.'

'Disgust?' he rasped, swinging round to face her. 'God Almighty, what sort of person do you take me for?'

'You needn't bother to deny it on my account,' retorted Maggie wearily. 'I'm not so sure that's not how I've been feeling about myself for the past three years.'

'That's criminal!' he exploded, striding over to tower in front of her. 'Feel disgusted with that bastard who did that to you, by all means. But why, in God's name, feel disgust with yourself?'

'I don't know... Perhaps that's not the right word... I've never been able to find the right words!' she exclaimed agitatedly. 'It's not as though I've ever blamed myself in any way for what Peter did to me... but somehow I couldn't handle what happened with you...and I just don't understand why. With you—a perfect stranger—everything had been as I'd dreamed it would be with him...yet after... I've never told a single soul what happened between us.'

He flung himself down on the sofa beside her. 'Of course you've never been able to find the right words,' he muttered hoarsely, his head tilted back against the cushions, his eyes closed. 'Two appalling experiences in one—'

'No!' she protested distractedly. 'You were never an appalling experience. Slane, you—'

'Maggie, I was a foreigner in a place where you knew no one and you were at your most vulnerable. Potentially our encounter could have turned out to be the most appalling experience of your life. You know as well as I do that I could have turned out to be anything, right up to an axe-wielding pervert—so don't try telling me you've never lost any sleep thinking along those lines.'

He groaned and gave an angry shake of his head. 'You learned all the right things about your sexuality through me, but the timing was so wrong it ended up doing you more harm than good. I should have been the guy some caring friend introduced you to some time after that bastard had treated you so badly... Maggie, how, in God's name, can you go on loving a subhuman like him?'

'Love him?' gasped Maggie. 'For heaven's sake, Slane, that's part of what I've been telling you. The very idea that I once even imagined myself in love with him makes me cringe with embarrassment.'

She rubbed her hands against her temples in an effort to clear her head of the confused images churning in it. 'Perhaps part of the reason I had such difficulty in being honest with you was to do with the fact that he had turned up in the shop out of the blue a few days before I went over to Dublin. Just the sight of him made me feel physically ill, but seeing him unsettled me far more than I was prepared to admit to myself.'

'And then you walked slap into me,' he stated grimly, then reached over and took one of her hands lightly in his. 'How much of all this does Connor know?'

'I never told him any details,' she replied, a bitter-sweet ache churning painfully through her as he raised her hand briefly to his mouth, as he had once before in

Dublin. 'I just let him think it was a romance gone wrong. I told Jim everything—and he wanted to kill Peter.'

'Why do you think I got up and walked away from you just now?' he asked almost wearily. 'Handling the idea that there's someone out there I'd gladly kill is something I've never had to do before.' He gave a bitter laugh. 'Though that's not the only thing I've learned I'm not up to handling in the past few weeks.'

He released her hand abruptly. 'You know, you really had me convinced there was this one and only love you were fixated on. . .though who am I to criticise you, when the only guy I wanted to free you to love was me?'

'You what?' she demanded dazedly, her mind still trying to digest his claim to wanting to kill Peter.

'Come on now, Maggie,' he drawled. 'You don't honestly think I was prepared to sit back and let some other guy snap you up?'

'I. . . What are you saying?' she croaked, shaking her head impatiently in an attempt to clear it. Then she glared at him as something at last clicked into place. 'With me in England and you in America, how did you plan on stopping it—telepathically?' she demanded witheringly.

'I guess this over-inflated ego of mine had me hoping you'd stop yourself.' His eyes met hers, inscrutable and unwavering. 'Perhaps I was just clutching at straws because of those times in the night when you would snuggle up to me and tell me you loved me. . . OK, so you said it in your sleep but. . .but that was when I believed in what turned out to be this fictitious love of your life.'

Maggie felt as though she was suffocating. 'There's

nothing fictitious about him,' she protested huskily, convinced that she had misunderstood what he was saying and had just made a terrible mistake. 'Perhaps he was semi-fictitious for a while. . . I honestly don't know what made me lie when you asked me if I'd ever been in love, because I hadn't.

'Then I started realising that once in my life I had experienced part of what I felt love should be. And when I told you I had made the mistake of falling in love with the wrong man. . .it was only half a lie.'

'There's no such thing as half a lie!' he exclaimed exasperatedly. 'Were you or weren't you in love with this monster who—?'

'No!' she howled. 'You talk about not being able to handle certain things. How was I supposed to be able to handle realising that the nearest I'd ever got to love was with a man with whom I'd had a one-night stand? The same man who now saw me as a cardboard cut-out of a real person, and who for a long time couldn't even bring himself to mention how we'd first met. The last thing I wanted was to end up loving him.'

'Having been there myself, I kind of know what you mean,' he sighed. 'Maggie, all those things I said and did—' He broke off, shaking his head. 'What I came here to find out is whether or not you ended up loving him.'

Maggie flashed him a murderously hostile look. 'If you think this is the way I behave normally, you need your head examined.'

'Oh, I need that all right,' he stated wryly. 'Maggie, it would make both our lives one hell of a lot easier if you could return to behaving normally. 'It's perfectly obvious that I love you, so what's your problem with loving me back?'

'Perfectly obvious?' she whispered in a voice croaking with disbelief. She'd thought *she* was half out of her mind—what, in God's name, was he?

'OK, so neither of us is too hot on spotting the obvious,' he stated in disconcertingly matter-of-fact tones. 'But think about it a while. Any minute now you'll see just how obvious it is.'

Maggie sank back against the armrest, her head spinning crazily. The only obvious thing was that any second now he would say something that would unsay everything he had just said, she warned herself confusedly.

'I didn't mean for you to take all day about it,' he groaned, reaching for her and hauling her into his arms.

Their mouths clung in an orgy of welcome, breaking off now and then to explore cheeks, chins and eyes as they poured out breathless chants of love. It was the laughter that began bubbling inexplicably in Slane and spilled infectiously into Maggie that finally drew them apart.

'This isn't funny,' she protested. 'Why are you laughing?'

'If it's not funny, why are you laughing?' He ducked his head to nibble her chin.

'Because. . .because I'm not right in the head! If you've just told me you love me after all you've put me through. . . God, I could *kill* you!'

'Go ahead and kill me,' he chuckled moistly in her ear, 'but it won't alter the fact that I love you. It took a long time for me to get my head around the fact that, had we met under any circumstances other than those we did three years ago, we'd probably be raising our own family now.'

'We would?' she croaked, praying that her lungs would start functioning again before she died from lack of breath.

'Wouldn't we?' he demanded huskily, leaning back to gaze down at her with eyes filled with unequivocal love. 'Or are you telling me you don't love me?'

'Of course I love you!' she exclaimed impatiently, then felt something glorious and indescribable break free within her. 'Oh, Slane. . . I can't believe I'm saying it! I love you!'

'About time too,' he complained contentedly, then shook her. 'Just making sure you're awake this time.' The wicked grin on his face faltered to a look almost of pain as he hugged her to him fiercely. 'God, the only time I felt sane in Dublin was when I had you safely in my arms. And when I think of how undecided I was about going there in the first place—' He broke off with a shudder.

'Yes, it must have been a wrench for you,' teased Maggie, utter happiness suffusing her, 'abandoning poor Felicity again.'

'Felicity,' he groaned. 'Now there's one terrifyingly determined woman. Thank God I'll have you to protect me from her.' He drew back again to look at her. 'You are going to protect me, aren't you, Maggie—for the rest of our lives?'

Once again her breathing apparatus let her down, and all she could do was cling to him in the hope that it would eventually sort itself out.

'If it's the breeding programme that's troubling you—forget it,' he pleaded softly. 'Though I must say the sight of you with Kieran's baby in your arms did things I'd never imagined possible to me.'

'I was pretty thrown by what it did to me, too,' choked Maggie, at last managing to get a breath.

'Those thoughts I was having that I shouldn't have been, the night before you abandoned me. . .?' he teased softly. 'Little Colm played a starring role in them. But I want to spend my life with you because I love you, and not for any children we might or might not have. You *are* my life, and don't you ever forget that.'

He placed a tender kiss on the end of her nose, then grinned down at her wickedly. 'So how about saying you'll be my wife as well as my life? Will you marry me?'

'Yes,' she whispered, joy exploding throughout her.

'You've just made me the happiest man alive,' he sighed, dropping his head to nuzzle his mouth against her neck. 'Which is pretty amazing, considering I never did get to sample your cooking.'

'Now I'm completely convinced you love me,' she chuckled, squirming as his persistent mouth sent soft shivers through her. She drew his head up to hers and began indulging in some exploration of her own.

'Uh-uh,' he protested, drawing back to gaze at her from darkly languorous eyes. 'You and I have a few calls we should make before we embark on what's going to be a lifetime of shenanigans. Your mother will need my shoe size and all those other endearing little details about me and— Maggie, stop looking at me like that!'

'I can't help it.' She laughed unsteadily, peeling herself from him.

'Where are you going?' he demanded in alarm.

'To get the phone. . .and to see if I can collect a few of my wits together while I'm getting it.'

'Any luck with the wits?' he asked, hauling her back into his arms when she returned a minute or two later.

'I didn't come across a single one,' she sighed dreamily. 'But maybe they'll turn up for my birthday. . .which happens to be tomorrow.'

'Tomorrow?' he exclaimed, cupping her face in his hands and gazing lovingly into her eyes. 'I guess the ring I intend getting you tomorrow won't count as a birthday present,' he murmured huskily. 'So what can I get you?'

'Nothing,' she whispered, linking her arms around his neck. 'I already have everything I could ever want.'

It was as his head began lowering purposefully towards hers that the telephone slid to the floor with a clatter.

Laughing, he jerked his head back from hers. 'Right,' he announced firmly. 'Your mom then mine, but, first of all, Connor. . . You realise he'll be claiming any credit there is for bringing us together, and that if we do have a child it'll have to be named after him?'

'And if it's a girl?' giggled Maggie.

'No problem—we'll call her Connora,' he replied. 'God, what a name.' He shuddered, laughing as he retrieved the telephone.

'You'd better make sure he's safely seated before you start saying anything,' warned Maggie, amazed to find that her heart hadn't yet burst with joy.

'Seated?' laughed Slane as he started dialling. 'I'll have to make sure the poor guy's horizontal before I can risk mentioning little Connora.'

GET 4 BOOKS
AND A MYSTERY GIFT

Return this coupon and we'll send you 4 Mills & Boon Romances and a mystery gift absolutely FREE! We'll even pay the postage and packing for you.

We're making you this offer to introduce you to the benefits of Reader Service: FREE home delivery of brand-new Mills & Boon Romances, at least a month before they are available in the shops, FREE gifts and a monthly Newsletter packed with information.

Accepting these FREE books and gift places you under no obligation to buy, you may cancel at any time, even after receiving just your free shipment. Simply complete the coupon below and send it to:

MILLS & BOON READER SERVICE, FREEPOST, CROYDON, SURREY, CR9 3WZ.

No stamp needed

Yes, please send me 4 free Mills & Boon Romances and a mystery gift. I understand that unless you hear from me, I will receive 6 superb new titles every month for just £2.10* each postage and packing free. I am under no obligation to purchase any books and I may cancel or suspend my subscription at any time, but the free books and gifts will be mine to keep in any case. (I am over 18 years of age)

1EP6R

Ms/Mrs/Miss/Mr _____

Address _____

_____

_____ Postcode _____

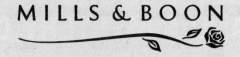

MILLS & BOON

Next Month's Romances

Each month you can choose from a wide variety of romance with Mills & Boon. Below are the new titles to look out for next month.

ONLY BY CHANCE	Betty Neels
THE MORNING AFTER	Michelle Reid
THE DESERT BRIDE	Lynne Graham
THE RIGHT CHOICE	Catherine George
FOR THE LOVE OF EMMA	Lucy Gordon
WORKING GIRL	Jessica Hart
THE LADY'S MAN	Stephanie Howard
THE BABY BUSINESS	Rebecca Winters
WHITE LIES	Sara Wood
THAT MAN CALLAHAN!	Catherine Spencer
FLIRTING WITH DANGER	Kate Walker
THE BRIDE'S DAUGHTER	Rosemary Gibson
SUBSTITUTE ENGAGEMENT	Jayne Bauling
NOT PART OF THE BARGAIN	Susan Fox
THE PERFECT MAN	Angela Devine
JINXED	Day Leclaire